Someone Knows
Her Secret . . .

The contents of the desk lay scattered on the floor. Along with pages torn from Felicia's schoolbooks. Her clothes. Her cassette tapes. Everything she owned.

Who did this? Who hates me so much?

Felicia picked up her favorite pullover shirt. Shredded.

I can't stay here. I can't stay in this room. She turned—and uttered a low moan of terror.

Dripping red letters covered the wall.

Is that blood? Felicia thought.

She focused on the message, struggling to read the smeared letters.

Her heart pounded in her ears as she realized what the message said.

RUNAWAY! GET OUT NOW! I KNOW EVERY-THING!

Books by R. L. Stine

FEAR STREET

FEAR STREET®
R·L·STINE

Runaway

A Parachute Press Book

AN ARCHWAY PAPERBACK
Published by POCKET BOOKS
New York   London   Toronto   Sydney   Tokyo   Singapore

This book is a work of fiction. Names, characters, places and
incidents are products of the author's imagination or are used
fictitiously. Any resemblance to actual events or locales or persons,
living or dead, is entirely coincidental.

AN ARCHWAY PAPERBACK *Original*

An Archway Paperback published by
POCKET BOOKS, a division of Simon & Schuster Inc.
1230 Avenue of the Americas, New York, NY 10020

ISBN: 0-671-52959-5

First Archway Paperback printing January 1997

10 9 8 7 6 5 4 3 2 1

FEAR STREET is a registered trademark of
Parachute Press, Inc.

AN ARCHWAY PAPERBACK and colophon are
registered trademarks of Simon & Schuster Inc.

Cover art by Bill Schmidt

Printed in the U.S.A.

IL 7+

Runaway

chapter

1

WELCOME TO SHADYSIDE, the sign read.

Felicia Fletcher trudged along in the late-afternoon gloom. Dark clouds hung low and heavy, threatening to drench her again.

"Shadyside," she whispered. Never heard of it.

She wiped her hands on her jeans. It didn't help. She was soaked. Her jeans heavy with rain. Her sneakers soft and squishy. Her brown ponytail dripping icy water down her back.

Felicia peered past the WELCOME sign. A bridge spanned a swiftly flowing river. The water swept crumpled leaves and twisted branches along.

Felicia shifted the heavy red backpack on her shoulders. She pulled her navy blue baseball cap lower over her blue eyes.

Shadyside. Felicia liked the name. Maybe I can be safe here, she thought. Maybe I can start over in Shadyside.

A lump rose in Felicia's throat. She didn't want to start over. She wanted to go home. Home where she had friends and people who cared about her.

But she couldn't. She couldn't ever go home. Not after what she did.

Don't start to cry again, Felicia, she ordered herself. You're soaking wet as it is. She turned and stared in the opposite direction. Should she try Shadyside—or keep moving?

Felicia wished she could forget what happened. Forget everything and everyone from the past. Start fresh.

But the memories would *never* disappear. The laboratory. The wires. The doctors.

Dr. Shanks especially.

His greasy gray beard and loud voice. Felicia remembered the first time she ever met him. They led her into the lab. The bright fluorescent lights hurt her eyes. They sat her down in a straight-backed wooden chair, the most uncomfortable chair she'd ever felt.

They crowded around her, working, working, working. A skinny man with glasses attached sticky electrodes to her temples. Green, black, red, blue, and yellow wires ran from the electrodes into a large computer terminal. The assistants barked orders back and forth.

"Trial run on module four," a gray-haired woman in a white coat called.

"Go module four," the skinny one with glasses replied. He flipped a switch, and one of the machines began a loud, rhythmic beeping. "Pulse is seventy-nine, blood pressure one-twenty."

"Is that good?" Felicia asked.

They ignored her. They always ignored her questions.

The skinny one with glasses moved a table in front of Felicia. Another assistant pushed in her chair.

"Tell Dr. Shanks that the subject is ready," the gray-haired woman ordered.

"My name is Felicia," she reminded them. "Why can't you ever use my name?"

The gray-haired woman regarded her coldly, saying nothing. She picked up a clipboard and began making notes.

"It's spelled F-E-L-I-C-I-A," Felicia grumbled.

The gray-haired woman stopped writing and stared at her.

"Did I go too fast?" Felicia asked sarcastically.

The woman set the pencil and clipboard down and left the room.

Seconds later, a bald man with a thick beard strode into the exam room, his white lab coat swishing with each step. He stood over six feet tall, with a large belly. He had a long, crooked nose, and deep-set eyes.

Angry eyes, Felicia thought. No laughter in there. Only a big, cold, dark nothing.

"Felicia," he said, folding his arms across his chest. "How are you today?"

3

"Fine."

"Fine. I am Dr. Shanks. I'm running this phase of the experiment. Unlike Dr. Cooper, I will not tolerate any sarcasm. You have to understand, Felicia. You are here to learn, but to teach as well. We need to learn from you. So you must clear your mind and concentrate. If you refuse to obey that one simple rule, you will be finished here at Ridgely College. Is that clear?"

A jolt of anger shot through Felicia. Who does this guy think he is? They need *me* a lot more than I need *them*.

Felicia gazed into Dr. Shanks's sunken eyes. He didn't turn away. He stared right back. "You need to learn to control your talents. If you don't, you will put others, and yourself, in danger."

Felicia shivered. "I understand," she finally replied.

"Fine. Let us begin." Dr. Shanks pulled a pencil from his coat pocket and placed it on the table in front of Felicia. "Move the pencil across the table, please."

"What?"

"Move the pencil across the table, please," Dr. Shanks repeated.

"I-I don't know if I can," Felicia stammered. She heard the machine's beeps increase with her heart rate. Her palms began to sweat.

"That is unacceptable," Dr. Shanks replied. "Move the pencil across the table, please."

"I can't just *do* it, you know!"

Dr. Shanks slammed his palm down on the table.

"What did I just explain to you? This is not a game. This isn't even a test. This is your *life*, young lady!"

"Don't yell at me!" she screamed. "I can't help it! I'm not one of your stupid machines! You can't just turn me on and off whenever you want! Get out of my face!"

Dr. Shanks drew in a deep breath. He leaned forward on the table, placing a hand on either edge. Leaned so close Felicia could feel his breath hitting her face. Smell the mix of onions and spearmint.

"Young lady, whether you know it or not, you are blessed with one of the most remarkable talents on the face of this planet. I advise you to cooperate and concentrate. If you don't, there are more important people who are waiting to see how your abilities work. And believe me, their tests will be much more painful than this. Is that clear?"

Felicia wanted to rip the itchy electrodes off her temples and run out of the lab. No, she told herself. I have to be strong. I have to try.

Because she knew Dr. Shanks wasn't lying. Her father had told her the same thing—a long line of doctors waited to put her strange talents to the test. Shanks would not be the worst.

She stared at the pencil.

"Concentrate," he ordered.

She focused on it. The pink eraser. The yellow paint. The sharp, black point.

In the background, the beeping grew faster. Felicia's heart hammered in her chest. Full of anger. Full of fear.

Do it, she told herself. *Just do it.*

5

"You're not concentrating!" Dr. Shanks whispered.

But she was. Felicia hurled all her energy toward the pencil. And she felt something.

Something growing inside her. Slowly inflating. Like a balloon.

"Concentrate," Dr. Shanks repeated. His voice dug deep into her brain.

Her power grew.

She pushed harder.

The machines beeped faster and faster. Felicia felt the blood rushing through her veins.

"Heart rate one-ten," came a voice from nowhere. "B.P. one-eighty."

Felicia's fingernails bit into her hands. The moisture on her palms could have been sweat—or blood.

"Concentrate," came the voice.

The doctor's voice. The enemy's voice.

Kill the enemy.

The power exploded in Felicia's mind. All at once the pencil became a part of her will. And she knew *exactly* what she wanted to do with it.

The pencil wiggled. Then it slowly turned around on the table, its point turning toward Dr. Shanks.

In her mind, Felicia took a strong grip on the pencil, squeezing it with all her might. The pencil stopped wiggling and rose several inches from the table. It hovered there, as if waiting for an order.

Now, she thought. *Do it!*

She made it happen. She forced all her anger, fear, and frustration into the shaft of the pencil.

She knew it was wrong. But she couldn't help herself.

Felicia aimed it at the only target she could see—and let loose with all her might.

Felicia cried out with the effort. It felt like throwing a giant spear. I did it! she thought. Yes!

Then she watched as the pencil rocketed across the room—toward Dr. Shanks's left eye.

chapter
_____

2

Felicia gagged and closed her eyes. She couldn't watch. Couldn't watch the pencil stab into Dr. Shanks's eye.

"Felicia!" Dr. Shanks howled.

She shook her head back and forth, her eyes shut tight.

"Felicia!" he called again. Hands grabbed her shoulders, holding her in the chair.

"No!" she screeched. "I didn't mean it! It just *happened!*"

"I know!" Dr. Shanks exclaimed. "Isn't it fascinating?"

What did he say? she thought.

"Open your eyes, Felicia," he urged, his voice full of excitement.

What was going on? Wasn't he in pain?

Felicia slowly opened her eyes.

Dr. Shanks stood before her—grinning. His eye was fine. No pencil stuck there. No blood and gore pouring down his face.

"Look what you did!" Dr. Shanks ordered. He pointed at the pencil embedded in the cork bulletin board behind him.

"What . . . ?" Felicia could barely speak.

"You nearly killed me!" Dr. Shanks cried. "Missed me by an inch! Isn't that amazing?"

A wave of relief swept over Felicia. She didn't kill him. She didn't kill him.

But I wanted to, Felicia thought. I *wanted* that pencil to tear into his eye.

Her stomach lurched at the thought. No! That couldn't be true. She wasn't a killer! It had to be the power. The power made her want to hurt and destroy.

The power was pure evil.

"Did you see how close you came to sticking me?" Dr. Shanks asked. His enthusiasm made Felicia sick. She almost killed him—and he was happy! "I knew you could do it. I knew it! Think what you could accomplish if you learned to control your telekinesis. Think of it!"

Telekinesis. Felicia shuddered at the word. It sounded like a disease, not the power to move objects with her mind. It wasn't wonderful, or a blessing. Her father was proof of that. The power brought nothing but misery. . . .

* * *

Felicia shook her head. Don't think about it, she told herself. The lab at Ridgely College is far away now.

And that's just the way she wanted it. No more experiments. No more electrodes. No more Dr. Shanks.

Now there was only Shadyside, and the future. All she had to do was walk across that bridge.

A car horn blared behind her. Felicia whirled, her eyes wide.

Bright headlights exploded in her vision. She heard the grinding sound of tires on gravel.

Felicia screamed.

The car sped right at her!

No time to dodge away, she realized.

No time to move!

chapter

3

The car roared toward her, its tires locked and skidding.

"Stop!" Felicia gasped. But the car kept coming.

A tidal wave of gravel sprayed up. Stinging her arms and legs.

The car ground to a halt inches in front of her. Felicia stood rooted in place, her whole body trembling.

Felicia stared at the car. She could hardly believe it hadn't hit her.

The car gleamed even in the gloomy light. Cherry red. And big. A GTO. The engine grumbled loudly. Angrily.

The passenger-side window rolled down. Felicia edged closer and peered inside.

"That's a good way to get yourself killed," came a deep voice from inside the car.

At first Felicia couldn't make out the driver. Then he leaned closer. He had red hair down to his shoulders and a thick, pointed goatee the same color. When he smiled, he revealed a mouthful of crooked teeth. "Two or three more inches and you'd be history."

"I-I'm sorry," Felicia stammered. Her heart pounded. "I didn't hear you coming."

The man raised one eyebrow and revved the engine. It growled in response.

"You didn't hear *this* engine?" he asked doubtfully.

Felicia shrugged. "I guess I was daydreaming."

The man's gaze ran up and down her shivering form. "You need a ride."

It was a statement, not a question.

A chill crept up Felicia's spine. Did she need a ride? Of course she did. She was freezing. Did she want a ride with this guy? She wasn't sure.

"Get in," he said.

"I don't know . . ."

"If you don't get in, then I won't apologize for almost hitting you. Bye."

He put the car in gear.

"Wait!"

The man turned, an expectant expression on his face.

Well . . . it is *really* cold, Felicia thought. "Okay," she finally replied. "Apology accepted."

"Cool," he muttered. "Plant yourself and let's go."

Felicia climbed in, sliding her backpack between her feet on the floor. The driver slammed his foot on the gas and the car leaped onto the bridge, tires squealing. He pushed the car even faster when they hit the paved road on the other side.

Felicia quickly strapped on her seat belt.

"You have a name?" the man asked.

"Felicia," she answered. She studied him as he drove. Cheeks heavily scarred from acne. Eyes set deep in their sockets. Arms thickly muscled. Tattooed strings of black barbed wire circled his forearms from the wrists to the elbows, with drops of painted blood running from the fake wounds.

This might be a big mistake, Felicia thought.

"My name's Lloyd," the man mumbled. "My friends call me Homicide." He grinned. "But you don't have to. Yet."

Felicia smiled back at him. I can't believe I got into a car with someone named Homicide, she thought. I better not get this guy angry. "That's cool. Why do they call you that?"

Lloyd cackled. "Because I'm a killer!"

Felicia froze.

"What?" she asked softly.

"Just a joke," Lloyd muttered.

Felicia smiled nervously. She didn't feel sure he was joking.

"Um, Lloyd?" Felicia swallowed. "Why don't you let me out here?"

She couldn't believe how calm she sounded. She felt terrified.

Lloyd glared at her. "Why?" he demanded.

"Well . . . I think it stopped raining. I want to walk."

"Hold on a second." Lloyd smoothed his goatee back into a sharp point. "I just want to get this whole thing crystal clear. You ask for my help, force me to offer it, act like you deserve it, and now you're throwing it back in my face? Pull over, Lloyd, I don't *need* you anymore." Lloyd sneered and Felicia shrank back against the car door.

"I'm sorry, Lloyd. I didn't mean to offend you. I didn't ask you to stop—"

"Liar. You *made* me stop this car!" Lloyd thrust his hand down under his car seat and grabbed a switchblade. *Click!* The shiny six-inch knife popped out.

"Lloyd!" Felicia screamed. "Put it down! Put it down, please!"

"Now you understand where I'm coming from," Lloyd replied. "Don't you?"

Felicia couldn't stop staring at the blade. Her hand crept toward the door handle, but the car was accelerating.

Too fast. We're going too fast for me to jump!

But she had to escape. Had to do something. Anything.

Oh no . . . I promise I will never hitchhike again. Ever ever again!

Felicia's heart slammed against her rib cage. Her breath caught in her chest.

"Lloyd?" she whispered. Her voice shook. "Why do you have a knife?"

He sneered at her and stomped harder on the gas pedal. The car sped up.

"Lloyd—stop!" Felicia cried. "What are you doing?"

"I gave you a ride," Lloyd told her. "Now you have to pay for it."

RUNAWAY

because the lid was tightly sealed, so he couldn't
smell the captive boy.

"I guess—I guess I have enough clothes on, now
done.

"Oh, there are lots of them around, Elicia," the
woman said.

chapter

4

"What are you talking about?" Felicia choked out.

Lloyd sneered at her. "You can get out, Felicia," he growled. "Just leave your wallet behind."

Felicia stared at him, astonished. "B-but I don't have any money," she stammered.

"Well, that's a shame," Lloyd said. "But then I guess I don't have to let you out of the car." He pulled back his arm, waving the knife's blade menacingly.

Felicia felt something stir inside her.

It built within her . . . the *power*.

Filling up like a balloon. Getting ready to explode.

Her fingernails dug into the upholstery and she sank deeper and deeper into the seat. She couldn't unleash it. Not here. Not now. Who knew what would happen?

The power grew. She couldn't control it much longer.

No! she thought desperately. *Force it back!*

But the image appeared in her mind. So clear and strong. The switchblade flying from Lloyd's hand into the backseat. Lloyd's palms slamming down on the steering wheel. Gripping it hard. Jerking it to the left. Steering the car into the other lane.

No! Don't let it happen! You'll die!

But she pictured it all: knife flying, car swerving, metal crumpling, glass shattering, blood everywhere.

It happened very fast.

With a flash of bright steel, the knife shot out of Lloyd's hand. Felicia heard Lloyd utter a startled cry. He jerked the wheel to the left. The car flew across the yellow line.

Felicia saw a tree looming bigger, bigger, bigger. *No! We'll die! We'll both die!*

Too late.

The car slammed full speed into the trunk of the tree!

The impact threw Felicia forward, the seat belt biting into her stomach.

Metal shrieked.

The windshield cracked.

Felicia's head slammed back against the seat. She tasted warm, salty blood in her mouth. My tongue, she thought. I bit my tongue.

Felicia could hear the steady rhythm of the

windshield wiper blades. Nothing else. Not a sound from the man beside her.

Slowly she opened her eyes.

She stared through the windshield at the hood of the car crumpled against the tree. The front end was ripped open. Steam hissed from the radiator.

Felicia turned to Lloyd. He lay slumped forward in his seat, a bright stream of blood running from a deep gash on his forehead. It flowed from his nose and chin and ran down the steering wheel. His arms hung limply. The barbed-wire tattoo looked more real than ever splattered with fresh blood.

Felicia shivered. Was he alive?

Cautiously she reached out and poked him in the ribs. Every muscle in her body tensed. She expected him to roar to life and lock his hands around her throat.

But he didn't move.

She leaned closer.

There—his chest rose. He's breathing, she thought. He's alive.

I didn't kill him.

But you *wanted* to kill him, an inner voice whispered. You killed once before—back in Ridgely. It's easy now. You know how easy it is to murder someone.

You wanted Lloyd to fly through the windshield and crush his skull on the trunk of that tree, and you almost made it happen. Didn't you?

It doesn't matter, Felicia told herself. He would have stabbed me if I didn't stop him.

Lloyd moaned.

Felicia had to get out of there. *Now.*

She popped her seat belt and pulled the door handle. The door wouldn't budge.

"Oh no," she whispered. "Come *on.*"

She threw her shoulder against the door. Nothing. She tried again, with more force. Nothing.

Then she remembered the window. It rolled down easily.

Felicia grabbed her backpack from the floor, pulled her baseball cap low, and crawled out. She surveyed the damage and shuddered.

The sound of a car caught Felicia's attention. She turned to the road and spotted a flash of light about half a mile away and coming fast. Headlights!

She bolted to the side of the road and waved her arms frantically. "Stop! Please stop!"

A groan came from the car. "Ooooohhh, what did you do?" Lloyd called. "What did you do?"

"Help me!" Felicia screamed. She waved her arms faster. "Help me, *please!*"

The headlights grew larger.

Lloyd's moans grew louder.

Felicia heard a thumping sound from the car. Lloyd wanted out, she knew. He wanted to come after her. If this car didn't stop for her . . .

She stepped out onto the road, into the car's path. *"Help me! Stop! You have to stop! Please!"*

"You made me wreck my car!" Lloyd groaned. "My beautiful car. *I'm going to kill you!"*

19

Panic shot through Felicia.

The car began to slow down in front of her.

"Thank you," Felicia whispered. "Thank you, thank you, thank you."

"I'll get you, Felicia," Lloyd called, sounding a little stronger.

Felicia glanced back at the wreck. Lloyd struggled to squeeze through the window. He would be out in seconds.

The other car stopped. Felicia sprinted to the passenger side and pulled the door handle. Locked.

"Open the door!" she wailed.

"Hold it," the driver ordered. He was a boy, about Felicia's age. "What's wrong? Do you need an ambulance?"

She stared at him in disbelief. She didn't have time for question-and-answer! Lloyd was halfway out his window.

"Please. *Open. The. Door.*"

The boy didn't move. "That guy needs help," he replied.

"Listen to me!" she yelled. "I hitched a ride with that guy and he tried to stab me!"

"You wrecked my car! I'll kill you!" Lloyd shrieked.

Felicia tried to stay calm. She looked into the driver's deep brown eyes. "He tried to take my money. I just grabbed the steering wheel and yanked," she explained. "I didn't know what else to do! You have to help me. He'll kill me!"

"Okay, okay," the boy replied. "Get in. We're out of here."

He opened Felicia's door and she scrambled inside. The tires squealed on the wet pavement as they sped away.

Felicia twisted in her seat to watch Lloyd through the rear window. His face twisted in fury as he shouted after her.

"Are you okay?" the boy asked.

"Yeah," Felicia replied. "Now I am."

She turned around in her seat and studied him for the first time. He had gentle brown eyes and a strong jaw. He hadn't shaved in a day or two.

"What happened back there?" he asked.

"I told you," Felicia replied. She couldn't get her hands to stop shaking. So she made fists.

"You hitched a ride with that guy?"

"Hey, it's cold out," she snapped. "I was soaked. I didn't have a whole lot of options."

"Hitchhiking is a pretty dumb thing to do," the boy replied. "No matter how cold you are."

"You think so?"

"Look what happened to you," he pointed out. "You don't know who could be a psycho-path."

"He called himself Homicide," Felicia said, shaking her head."

"No way!" the boy replied. "Homicide?"

"Yeah. That's when I knew I was in trouble."

"Well, you're okay now," he said. "My name is Nick. Just Nick."

Felicia smiled. "Is that your nick-name?"

He chuckled.

She held out her hand. "I'm Felicia."

"Pleased to meet you, Felicia." Nick shook her hand, his grip warm and firm. "Guess you're having a bad day."

"Guess I'm having a bad year," Felicia muttered.

Nick looked surprised. "Is it really that bad?"

"I don't want to talk about it, okay?"

Nick held up his hand. "Okay, okay. Sorry."

Felicia felt bad. She didn't mean to snap at him. Nick made her feel comfortable. She *wanted* to tell him about herself. But she couldn't. Not if she wanted to stay safe.

Felicia could never tell anyone about her powers. Or what happened that horrible day in Ridgely.

"Do you want to go to the police?" Nick asked as they drove along the River Road into Shadyside.

"No!" she blurted out, much louder than she intended.

Don't make him suspicious.

"But that guy attacked you," Nick argued.

"Yeah, but I'm fine. He got his."

"Okay," Nick said reluctantly. "It's your call."

"Thanks." Felicia glanced over at Nick again. She wished she were an ordinary high-school girl. Riding home after a date with Nick.

Whoa. Where did that idea come from?

Well, Nick is really cute, she thought. And he saved me from that crazy guy.

But she couldn't trust him. She couldn't trust anyone.

The piercing wail of a siren interrupted Felicia's

22

thoughts. She spun in her seat. Spinning red, white, and blue lights flashed behind them.

Her heart leaped into her throat.

The police!

They found her!

chapter
5

"Wow! They're really moving," Nick commented over the howl of the siren.

Felicia's body went rigid. *They can't be on to me that fast. No way! Unless . . .*

Unless Felicia's picture was all over every police computer in the state!

The spinning lights grew larger in the rear window, the siren screaming.

"I wasn't speeding!" Nick growled. "What do they want?"

"Can't you lose them?" Felicia pleaded.

"Are you insane? I'm pulling over." He eased the car over to the curb, and the police cruiser closed in on them.

This is it, Felicia thought. *I'm going to jail. They know all about the deaths, and they've got me.*

The police car roared past them. At the next intersection, it turned right. The siren grew faint.

"Ha!" Nick smiled. "I knew I didn't do anything wrong," he said as he made a left turn.

Felicia let out a sigh. False alarm.

Nick pulled back onto the street and they continued on. Felicia tried to orient herself, searching for landmarks and street signs and anything else that would give her information she could use later.

She thought ahead all the time. Trying to prepare for the next time she had to lie her way out of a sticky situation. Sometimes she hated herself for lying. But it kept her out of prison, didn't it?

"What's this town like, Nick?"

Nick shrugged. "I don't know. Like any other town, I guess. Too small."

Felicia nodded.

"Um, Felicia?"

"Yeah?"

"I know it's probably not my business. . . ." He hesitated. "Do you have a family around here?"

Felicia stiffened. She thought of her father. Her Aunt Margaret. All the good times. So far away.

"You're right, Nick," she replied coldly. "It's not your business."

"Hey, sorry," he muttered. "But if you're in some kind of trouble . . ."

"What do you mean?"

"Come on, Felicia. You're hitching rides in the pouring rain. You won't talk about your family. And you nearly had a heart attack when the cops passed us." Nick's eyes narrowed. "You're a runaway."

"You don't know anything," Felicia shot back.

"Tell me I'm wrong," Nick challenged.

"Drop it."

"I want to help, okay?"

What a sweet guy, Felicia thought. But she couldn't let him get too close. "Thanks, but you've done enough already," she replied.

"Fine," Nick answered.

They rode in silence for several blocks.

I hurt his feelings, Felicia realized. She had to say something.

"Nick, I mean it. You really have helped me so much," she told him softly. "I'll never be able to repay you. But if you want to help, you have to forget you ever met me. It's important."

She spied a little shop coming up on the right. The Donut Hole. "Let me out here," she instructed.

"Felicia—"

"No. Really. Let me out, Nick."

"Okay, okay." He pulled over and put the car in park. "Look. I don't care why you ran away. If you need anything—"

"No, Nick," she interrupted. "Believe me, I'll be fine." She smiled at him.

If only I could have met him some other time, she thought. Some other place. Some other life . . .

Felicia couldn't help herself. She leaned over and kissed him lightly on the lips. "Thanks."

He blinked in surprise. "You're welcome."

Felicia grinned, then her smile faded. "Remember, the best thing you can do for both of us is forget all about me."

She grabbed her backpack and opened the door.

"How am I supposed to forget about you after you kissed me?" Nick grumbled.

"You seem like a smart guy, Nick," she replied. "You'll figure it out."

Before he could say anything more, Felicia slammed the car door, turned, and strode into the Donut Hole.

She didn't look back.

Felicia headed straight to the bathroom. She changed into dry clothes. She combed out the tangles in her hair, wishing she had a blow-dryer. Then she re-tied her ponytail and put her baseball cap back on.

The dry clothing felt wonderful. She walked back into the donut shop and ordered a toasted bagel and coffee. She took her food to the booth farthest from the door—and the other customers. She pulled her hat low.

No one noticed her at all.

Perfect.

Now that she had time, Felicia wanted to figure out what to do next. She didn't have a place to stay. And the few dollars in her pockets wouldn't keep her eating much longer.

The bottom line: she needed a job. Where to begin? She sighed and took a bite of her bagel.

Then Felicia caught a piece of conversation between two teenagers in the next booth.

"I can't believe I did it. This is going to destroy our whole vacation," one boy moaned. "I totally forgot."

"You are such an idiot, Bobby," the second boy

said. "How long have we planned this trip? How could you forget about it?"

"I needed the money. Dr. Jones gave me a hundred bucks up front. How could I refuse?"

"I think you offered to watch his house over on Fear Street and feed his mangy cat because of your grade," the second boy accused. "You think now he'll give you a B-plus instead of a B-minus."

Bobby chuckled. "Well, maybe."

"I can't believe you," the second boy continued. "You can't find anyone to do this cat-sitting job?"

Felicia smiled to herself. It's about time something went right for me, she thought. I can get everything I need from these guys.

It can work—but you'd better be convincing, she warned herself. Felicia took a deep breath. Now or never. She turned around and leaned into their booth.

chapter

6

"*E*xcuse me," Felicia interrupted. "Are you talking about Dr. Jones, the college professor?"

"Yeah," the guy named Bobby replied. He had three days of stubble on his face, and a baseball cap that sat backward on his head. "What's it to you?"

"I know him," she said brightly. "My father is good friends with him. If you want, I could watch his house for you."

"Really?" the second guy piped up. He wore his hair in ragged spikes and had Greek letters on his T-shirt. "Take it, Bobby, and let's hit the road."

"Hold it," Bobby replied. "I'm not just going to hand over Dr. Jones's keys. How do I know you really know Dr. Jones?"

"Because I do," Felicia replied.

The second guy grinned. "I like her, Bobby. Just give her the keys."

Bobby's eyes narrowed. "You know where his house is?"

"Over on Fear Street, right?"

"Yeah, number six twenty-seven."

"Come on, Bobby," the second guy urged.

"Hold on a minute!" Bobby snapped. He glared at Felicia. "Dr. Jones is gone for at least a month. He's on safari or something. He asked me to check the house every day, feed the cat, and water the plants. You think you can handle it?"

"Yeah." Felicia rolled her eyes. "I think I can handle it."

Bobby reached into his pocket and tossed Felicia a single key. "Don't mess this up for me," he warned.

"I know, I know," Felicia replied. "Your B-plus is riding on it."

"All right, man!" the second guy yelled. "Let's hit the road! Come on!" They slid out of the booth and headed for the door.

Felicia cleared her throat loudly. "Bobby?"

He stopped and glared back at her. "Now what?"

"Well, I think I heard you say that Dr. Jones gave you a hundred bucks up front before he left?"

He frowned. "What about it?"

"Give me fifty, and your worries are over. Kitty-cat won't starve."

"Fifty?"

"If a big smart college guy is worth a hundred, I figure a high-school girl is worth fifty, don't you?"

"You have to be kidding!" Bobby protested.

"Give her the money, man," his friend urged. "Let's *go.*"

"Think about it, Bobby," Felicia pointed out. "You're still getting fifty bucks for doing nothing."

Bobby shook his head. But he reached into his pocket and fished out several crumpled bills. He dropped them on the table in front of her.

"I'll be back in two weeks," he said. "Leave the key in the mailbox so I can pick it up." He turned to go, then paused. "By the way, what's your name?"

"Felicia," she said quickly. "Felicia Smith."

"Uh huh," he replied. "Thanks, Felicia Smith. I owe you one."

"Forget it. You paid me."

Bobby nodded, and the two guys strode out of the Donut Hole.

Felicia slipped back down into her booth and smiled. I am *so* smooth, she thought.

Felicia found Dr. Jones's house with no problems. The large, gray Victorian mansion sat far back from the street. She walked up the steps to the porch and peered in the front window. She couldn't see much.

Felicia slid the key into the lock and opened the front door. It swung wide on creaky hinges. She stepped inside slowly.

A big gray tabby cat meowed a greeting. Felicia picked the cat up and checked her I.D. tag. "Miss Quiz," Felicia read aloud. Strange name for a cat.

This cat has to weigh at least fifteen pounds,

Felicia thought. I bet she brings home large dead rodents in her mouth and leaves them on the back porch as a surprise.

Miss Quiz sniffed Felicia and offered a soft purr. Felicia set the cat back down. She locked the front door and checked all the other doors. Then she checked the windows and pulled all the shades.

When she felt convinced the house was secure, she returned to the den. She slumped down in Dr. Jones's reading chair and smiled at Miss Quiz sitting across the room. "I'll be safe here with you, right, kitty?"

Miss Quiz stared back at her, yellow eyes unblinking.

Felicia shivered. How could she feel safe in a place called Fear Street?

Felicia showed up at Shadyside High early the next morning. She marched into the office with confidence, and told her biggest lie yet.

The secretary registered her with a smile. She didn't even question it when Felicia explained that the transcripts from her previous school were "on the way."

Within an hour Felicia had an armful of books and a full class schedule. Felicia managed to open the combination lock on her locker on the first try. She stashed the books she wouldn't need until after lunch. Then she pulled a worn, wrinkled picture of a handsome older man out of her backpack. She smiled.

Dad.

She taped the photo inside the locker, then

slammed the door shut. She moved off to her first class.

It felt so good to slip back into a normal life again. Become part of the crowd. Just another ordinary high-school kid. Felicia loved every second of her first day.

After her last class ended, Felicia dumped her books in her locker and headed for the front doors. She caught sight of a guy staring at her from down the hall.

Her heart started to beat faster. Oh no. Why is he staring? *Does he know who I am?*

chapter

7

*F*elicia shot another glance at the boy. Dark hair, brown eyes.

Nick!

Felicia let her breath out in a *whoosh* as he hurried over to her.

"What are you doing here?" he demanded.

He's even cuter than I remembered, Felicia thought. "I'm . . . well, I'm going to school here now," she managed to reply. "Is there something wrong with that?"

"No way!" Nick exclaimed. "In fact, it's the best news I've heard all day. I guess this means everything's cool with you? I mean, about yesterday and everything."

Felicia nodded. "I worked some things out. Shadyside is home for now."

"For now," Nick repeated.

Neither of them said anything for a long moment. Felicia couldn't take her eyes away from Nick's. "Stop staring. Don't you know it's rude?" she teased.

"Hey, you started it."

"There's a clock above your head," Felicia explained. "I wanted to know what time it was."

"Yeah, right."

Felicia pointed at the other wall. Nick glanced over his shoulder—and saw the clock. "Oh," Nick muttered.

Felicia burst out laughing.

"Gee, thanks," Nick growled. "I think I'll go now."

"Oh, don't be a baby," Felicia said as they wandered outside.

"Which way are you headed?" he asked.

"Fear Street," Felicia replied.

A strange expression crossed Nick's face.

"What?" Felicia asked.

"Nothing," he replied quickly, not meeting her eyes.

Felicia didn't buy that. *"What?"* she repeated.

"A lot of things have happened on that street. Horrible things."

I bet I can top them all, Felicia thought.

"It seems normal enough," she commented.

"I guess," he mumbled. "Hey, how about a hamburger?"

"I'd love it," Felicia replied. But don't let him get too close, she reminded herself. You can't go spilling your guts to some stranger—even if he seems like a great guy.

"I'll even cook it for you," Nick promised.

"You cook?" Felicia teased.

"Yeah. I work part time at the Burger Basket."

"Cool."

As they walked, Felicia asked Nick questions about school. She made sure their conversation didn't get too personal.

When they arrived at the Burger Basket, Nick led Felicia back behind the counter and into the kitchen. A blond guy refilling catsup and mustard containers grinned at Nick. "I'm saving the mayonnaise for you," he called. "I hate that stuff."

A tall, skinny man with a flat-top haircut, wearing a white shirt and black tie, marched out from a back room. "Hey, Nick!" he barked. "Get the lead out, man. You're late!"

"Sorry, Barry," Nick responded. "I got hung up."

"So I see," Barry replied. "I want two dozen burgers cranked for the dinner rush. Move it."

"I'm on it." Nick slid out of his backpack and gestured at Felicia. "This is Felicia."

"Ah, Felicia." Barry nodded. "The hitchhiking damsel in distress."

"So Nick bragged about what a hero he was?" Felicia guessed.

"Yeah, he told me all about it when he stopped in for his usual breakfast burger this morning," Barry replied. "He said he took on four guys to save you."

"Four, huh?" Felicia replied. "He wishes."

"Four guys, Barry. I'm not kidding," Nick said with a smile.

"Quit while you're ahead," Barry warned. "And get into your uniform. I want those burgers ready."

Nick headed off to the rest room. Okay, Felicia thought. Now's your chance.

"Any job openings?" she asked Barry.

Barry folded his arms across his chest. He studied her. He didn't reply.

"I need the money," Felicia added.

Barry stroked his bony chin. "You ever work a grill before?"

"Yeah, at a Hamburger Hut," Felicia replied.

Another big, fat lie, she thought. But how hard can it be? I'll just copy what everyone else is doing.

"How about this," Barry said. "Stop in tomorrow. I'll try to get you a shift this weekend. Will you work nights?"

She needed to work as many hours as possible so she could afford a place to stay when the house-sitting deal was over. "Any place, any time," Felicia replied. "And I won't be late like Nick."

"Hey, I heard that," Nick complained. He strode toward them in an orange and brown uniform.

"I'm going to be working here," Felicia told him. "So you can walk me here tomorrow—in case those *four* guys show up again!"

"Sounds good," Nick mumbled. He pulled on an orange visor.

"Yeah." Barry chuckled. "Zan will *love* that."

Nick glared at his boss.

"Who's Zan?" Felicia asked.

.*"I'm* Zan," came a cold, stern voice from behind Felicia.

Felicia turned. A slim girl with long black hair and bright blue eyes stood in the doorway. She held a head of lettuce in one hand and a huge carving knife in the other.

Uh-oh, Felicia thought. This must be Nick's girlfriend. I bet that's his class ring on the chain around her neck.

"Zan," Nick said quickly. "This is Felicia. She's the one I told you about."

"Oh, yeah," Zan nodded. "The hitchhiker. I'm Zan. It's short for Alexandria." Zan smiled. "I'm so glad you're okay. Who knows what would have happened if Nick hadn't come along."

"I know," Felicia replied awkwardly.

"Felicia is going to be working here too," Barry announced. Then he pointed at Nick. "Burgers. And send Kevin on his break. I want him back before the rush."

Nick hurried over to the grill. A moment later the blond guy ambled past them. He poured himself a soda and headed out the back door.

"Hey, Barry," the kid behind the register called. "I have an overring."

Barry fished a key out of his pocket and hurried over to the front counter. Leaving Zan and Felicia alone.

Felicia struggled to come up with something to say. "Um, so how long have you worked here?" she asked.

Zan didn't answer. She studied Felicia.

Felicia felt the hairs on the back of her neck

prickle. She wished Zan would stop staring at her like that. Her icy blue eyes gave Felicia the creeps.

Zan marched up to Felicia. She raised the butcher knife in her hand.

Pointed it at Felicia's chest.

A gasp escaped Felicia's lips. She stumbled backward, her eyes locked on the gleaming blade.

chapter

8

Zan advanced. "You might owe Nick your life," Zan said, her voice flat and cold. "But he's going with me. Remember that."

Felicia felt her power swell inside her. No, she thought. Don't let it out. Not here. She took another step back—and banged into the wall.

Zan swung the knife down at Felicia.

"Whoa!" Nick screamed.

Zan laughed and lowered the knife to her side. "Hey, Felicia. It was just a joke," she said. "I've got to slice some lettuce." She waved with the knife still in her hand.

Felicia couldn't speak. She needed all her concentration to control her power. She tuned out the sounds of the restaurant. Tuned out the sounds of

Nick and Zan talking. She willed the power back inside her.

But the power kept growing. It's going to blow, Felicia thought.

The power burst out. Felicia forced it away from herself. Away from Zan and Nick and Barry. Away from all the people in the building.

The french fry vat began bubbling and hissing. Spraying hot oil onto the floor. A stack of wet trays toppled off a counter. The lights flickered.

"What's going on?" Barry yelled.

Felicia took a deep breath as the last of the power flew out. It's okay, she told herself. It's over—and you didn't hurt anybody.

"Weird," Nick cried. "I think we blew a fuse. We still need some replacements," he reminded Barry. "We shouldn't be using the wrong size."

"I'll pick some up," Barry promised. "Now back to work."

Zan turned to face Felicia. "I'm sorry I scared you. I really was just kidding around."

"No problem," Felicia replied. "But I don't like knives."

"Oh wow, I forgot!" Zan moaned. "That creep in the car pulled a knife on you, didn't he?"

"Yes," Nick snapped.

"Wow, I am *so* sorry," Zan repeated. "Really."

Felicia smiled. "It's okay."

"Come on, guys," Barry barked. "Fun time is over. Felicia, I expect to see you here tomorrow."

"Thanks, Barry," Felicia said.

Nick made her a burger to go. "See you guys tomorrow," she called as she headed out.

That was way too close, Felicia thought as she started home. My power almost got away from me. Something terrible could have happened.

The way it did in Ridgely.

"Hey, Felicia! Sit over here."

Felicia spotted Zan waving to her from a table in the back of the lunchroom. Nick sat beside her.

Felicia carried her tray over to the table and sat down across from her friends.

"Nice to eat a burger that someone else cooked, huh?" Nick asked.

"No kidding." Felicia squeezed some catsup onto her hamburger. "By nine o'clock last night I felt ready to pass out."

"I'm glad you showed up when you did," Zan said. "We never have enough people on weekends."

Felicia had worked shifts at the Burger Basket on Saturday and Sunday. It was hot, messy work, but she didn't care. Barry and Nick kept her laughing, and Zan had turned out to be pretty cool.

"Is the Basket much different than Hamburger Hut?" Nick asked. He mashed his fork into his chicken potpie, creating a brown-green pool of goop on his plate.

"Uh, not really," Felicia answered. She wrinkled her nose as she watched Nick continue mangling his food. "Are you really going to eat that?"

"In a minute," he told her. "It's not ready yet."

"Nick isn't happy until he's sure it's dead," Zan whispered to Felicia. They both laughed.

"It looks like something he ate an hour ago. Not something he's *about* to eat!" Zan joked.

Nick mashed his food even harder.

"It's not as bad as what he did with the leftovers from the salad bar yesterday." Zan shook her head.

At work Nick used the food to make all kinds of sick jokes. Felicia loved his twisted sense of humor.

"I can't believe the stuff Barry let's you get away with," Zan added.

"What can I say? I'm his star burger-burner."

"And Felicia is the rookie of the week," Zan said.

"Totally," Nick agreed. He raised his Coke high in the air.

"Don't pour that on my food!" Zan cried.

Felicia covered her burger with both hands.

"A toast," Nick explained. "To Felicia, the newest member of the hamburger team."

Zan clapped, and they all took a swallow of soda.

"Thank you, thank you!" Felicia cried as if accepting an Academy Award.

It felt so good to have friends again, people to hang out with. As long as she didn't let them get too close.

As long as she didn't do anything to hurt them.

After her last class, Felicia stopped by her locker and dumped her books. She finished all her homework in study hall, so she didn't have to lug anything home.

Cool, she thought. No *home*work. No *work* work. I'm going to find an old movie on TV and make a big bowl of popcorn. The perfect night.

Well, almost perfect, she admitted to herself. Nick won't be there.

Stop torturing yourself, she thought. He's off-limits. He's a friend's boyfriend. And that's that.

She started to slam the locker shut when she noticed an envelope taped to the inside of the door. Right next to the picture of her dad.

She yanked it off. It was blank.

Strange, she thought. She tore the envelope open and pulled out a single sheet of folded paper. Part of it appeared to be burned. Charred flakes littered the bottom of the envelope.

Felicia unfolded the sheet of paper—and gasped.

Someone had scribbled a note in orange marker:

I KNOW ALL ABOUT YOU!

Felicia felt a wave of nausea sweep over her. She leaned against her locker.

This couldn't be happening.

Below the note was a crystal-clear photocopy of Felicia's driver's license.

With her *real* name.

And her address in Ridgely.

A hot, sour taste hit the back of Felicia's throat as she stared down at the photo on the license.

Her face . . .

Her face had been burned away.

chapter

9

*F*elicia's hands began to shake. Someone knows who I am. Someone knows my last
name is Fletcher, not Smith. Someone knows I'm
from Ridgely.

But who?

Who?

Felicia felt a burst of energy rocket through her.
The power! She could feel it growing.

No! she told herself. You have to stop it. You
can't let it out again.

But she couldn't control it. It grew too fast.

The row of lockers in front of her began to
tremble. The metal doors rumbled and clanged
against their locks.

Thunk! Thunk! Thunk! Books slammed against
the locker doors.

Felicia's locker door went berserk! Slamming open and shut, open and shut, open and shut.

Felicia threw her weight against the door and forced it closed. She could feel the metal straining against her.

She dug her feet into the floor. Struggling to keep the door shut.

Bang! It sprang free.

Felicia dropped to her knees. She huddled on the floor with her hands over her ears. Trying to block out the horrible clanking and thumping sounds.

A surge of anger swept through her. She shoved herself to her feet. "Stop it!" she screamed. "Stop it! I control you. You *don't* control me!"

Seconds later, the lockers stilled. The hall became silent again.

Felicia scanned the hall. Did anyone see what happened?

No. No one there.

Good thing I took my time after class, Felicia thought. It gave everyone a chance to clear out.

Felicia shut her locker door. She snapped the lock closed and gave the knob a twirl.

Then she stuffed the frightening note into her backpack and sprinted out through the front doors.

Felicia slowed down when she reached the sidewalk. Could someone be following me? Does the person who sent that note know I live on Fear Street? They knew which locker was mine.

She forced herself to act naturally. She wandered through town, pretending to window-shop. Every block she would glance behind her. Trying to spot someone sticking with her.

No one.

When Felicia reached the Donut Hole, she decided to go inside. She ordered a soda and took it to a booth by the window.

No one here knows the truth, Felicia told herself as she stared out the window. Even if someone found out her real name, that didn't mean they knew everything about her past. That didn't mean they knew the reason she had to leave Ridgely.

What should she do now? Should she run away again? Move on to a different town? Or should she risk staying in Shadyside where she had a job and a place to live?

And Nick, she thought. But I don't really have him, do I?

Felicia wished she could talk everything over with someone. Really *talk*. And she knew only one person she trusted to listen.

I could call him, Felicia thought. I could call Nick. That's no big deal. That's not trying to steal Zan's boyfriend.

Felicia rushed over to the pay phone and dialed the Burger Basket. Barry answered and got Nick for her without asking any questions.

"Hey, what's up?" Nick asked cheerfully. Felicia could hear someone placing a drive-thru order in the background.

"Uh, nothing . . . I guess." Good, Felicia, she joked to herself. But it felt harder than she thought to talk about herself—even to Nick.

"It doesn't sound like nothing." Nick paused. "What's the matter?"

"Is Zan there?" she asked.

"Nope," Nick replied. "She's off today."

"Oh." Maybe this is a stupid idea, Felicia thought. It's safer not to talk to him. Safer for me . . . and for Nick.

"Felicia, whatever it is, you can talk to me, you know." Nick sounded worried.

Felicia sighed. "I guess that's why I called."

"It's slow right now. I'll convince Barry to give me my break early," Nick replied. "Where are you?"

Felicia hesitated a moment. "The Donut Hole," she answered.

"Nick, you on vacation or something?" she heard Barry yell.

"Barry's having a cow. I've got to go, but I'll be there soon." Nick hung up.

Felicia returned to her booth. About fifteen minutes later Nick strode in. He didn't even take time to change out of his uniform, Felicia noticed.

Nick plopped down across from her. "What happened?" he asked immediately.

"Nothing really . . . I mean, I guess I'm afraid."

"Of what?"

Felicia wanted to tell Nick everything. But she couldn't risk it.

I'll tell him a little, she decided. Just a little. She took a deep breath, then began. "You and Zan are the first friends I've had in a while," she admitted. "Things are going really well for me in Shadyside, and I'm . . ."

"What?" Nick prodded gently.

"I'm afraid that I'm going to lose everything," she replied softly. "I'm afraid I'll have to leave."

"Why? You just got here," Nick protested.

"I can't help it, Nick!" Felicia tried to keep her voice down. She couldn't let her emotions get out of control. "I'm a runaway, and that's what I do. I run!"

Nick grabbed her hand and squeezed it.

"So, stop running," he stated. "I don't know what's chasing you. Either you will tell me or you won't. But it doesn't matter. I'm still your friend. So is Zan. We don't want you to leave."

Felicia stared down at the table. Nick wouldn't say that, she thought, if he knew the terrible thing I did.

"I don't want to leave," she whispered. She gazed into his eyes. "I like it here."

"So stay," Nick replied. "Whatever it is, I'll be here for you. I promise."

Felicia smiled. "Why are you being so nice to me, Nick? You don't know anything about me."

He shrugged. "I don't know."

"Good answer," Felicia muttered.

They laughed. Felicia hadn't told him much, but she felt better.

Maybe I *can* stay, she thought. But I need to find out who sent that note. I need to find out how much they know.

"It's getting late," Nick said. "I have to get back or Barry will have a fit. Are you going to be okay?"

Felicia nodded. "Thanks for coming, Nick. It really means a lot."

Nick stood up. "You want a ride . . . some-where?" he asked. "Barry can wait a few more minutes."

"No," Felicia said quickly. "I'm going to hang out here awhile."

"Okay," he replied. "Maybe some day I'll see where you live."

"Maybe," she answered. But probably not, she added silently.

Felicia climbed out of the booth. She gave Nick a hug. He hesitated, then returned it.

Nick stepped back. "Bye," he mumbled. He headed for the door.

Felicia took a deep breath. She had a lot to think about. But at least she knew Nick would be there for her. And Zan too.

They were her friends. Her only friends.

I'll never let anything happen to them, she vowed.

And I'll never hurt them . . . the way I hurt Andy and Kristy.

I'll never use my power that way again. My power to kill.

chapter
10

Ridgely

"Dr. Shanks keeps pushing me harder and harder," Felicia complained to her friend Debbie Wilson. "He scares me sometimes—he's so intense."

Felicia and Debbie strolled along the beach not far from Ridgely College. The sand felt so good between Felicia's toes. After hours in the lab, she needed a long walk on the beach to keep sane.

"Dr. Shanks hardly pays any attention to me," Debbie said. "I should just resign from the experiment. It's as if he thinks I'm a waste of his time."

"You're lucky," Felicia told her.

Debbie ran her hands through her short blond hair, making it curlier than ever. *"I'm* lucky?" Debbie cried. "You have this amazing gift, and you're afraid to use it. I—"

Felicia picked up a shell and threw it into the ocean. "You think it's so wonderful and exciting. But I hate it! I don't want to spend my life being studied by a bunch of doctors."

"Why don't you go somewhere else?" Debbie suggested. "You hate your aunt. You hate Ridgely."

"I couldn't do that to Aunt Margaret. She's taken care of me since my dad died," Felicia explained. "She treats me as if I were her own daughter."

"But you don't get along," Debbie pointed out.

"Sure we do. Sometimes."

"You call all that arguing 'sometimes'?" Debbie asked.

"Come on, Debbie. Everyone fights. It's life."

"I wouldn't put up with it for a second," Debbie insisted.

"Well, you're not me, okay?" Felicia snapped.

"Okay, okay. So how many pencils did you shoot at Dr. Shanks today?" Debbie asked, changing the subject.

Felicia sighed. "None. He got so angry! But I couldn't find the power today."

"I wish I could find it even once." Debbie sighed.

"It's not so great," Felicia told her. "Who cares about dumb telekinetic powers? You're really smart. That's more important."

"I'm smarter than most of the doctors testing me," Debbie agreed. "But a lot of people are smart." She kicked some sand. "No one can do what you do. You're special."

They passed an old abandoned beach house. Most of its windows broken. Most of its shingles missing.

"I hate that house," Felicia declared. "It's so ugly."

"So tear it down," Debbie suggested.

"I can't knock that house down!" Felicia exclaimed. "Are you nuts?"

"I would," Debbie said. "If I had the power, I would have fun with it. I wouldn't stand around whining all the time."

Felicia grew angry. Debbie always got this way when they talked about Felicia's power. Debbie was jealous, bottom line.

Debbie has everything going for her, Felicia thought. Guys love her curly blond hair, her pretty face, her full lips. She's smarter than everyone in school.

But Debbie wanted the power, the only thing she couldn't have.

Felicia wondered why Debbie joined in the long, torturous experiments when she didn't show signs of any power. Did she hope she would develop it? Not likely. Felicia's father said Felicia had the power at birth. Just as he had.

"Forget it," Debbie finally said. "You probably couldn't even dent that house anyway. It's a lot bigger than a pencil."

I hate her when she's like this, Felicia thought. Hate her!

She reached deep down within herself, using the hot energy of her anger. And she found the power.

Felt it.

Caressed it.

She gave Debbie a grin. "You just watch me," she said.

Felicia turned toward the house. She concentrated, felt all the anger churning within her. She felt the power surging up with every heartbeat.

Soon the picture became clear in her mind. The roof caving in. The wooden walls splintering. The chimney crumbling in a cloud of red brick dust. The whole house falling apart.

And I'm the hammer, Felicia thought. She *shoved* the power out. Aiming at the house.

Beads of sweat formed on her forehead and rolled down her face.

More, she thought. *More.*

She heard a groan from the house. A blast of adrenaline shot through her. It's working! I'm doing it!

One of the windows cracked. Another exploded, glass flying in all directions.

Nails squealed as they flew out of the wood planks.

Every muscle in Felicia's body hummed. All the power inside her broke free and thundered toward the house.

The house shuddered violently. Then it came down all at once. Glass flying. Wood splitting. Plaster crumbling into powder.

Felicia felt exhilarated . . . and terrified.

It's too much power—too much power!

"What's that?" Debbie cried.

Felicia listened. Screams.

Screams from inside the house. Inside the crumbled, twisted wreck.

The two girls sprinted up the dunes as fast as they could.

Then Felicia froze.

"Oh no." Felicia's stomach twisted into knots. "No, no, no." She pointed at two cars that had been hidden behind the house.

Debbie's face went pale. "Those are Andy and Kristy's cars!" Debbie whispered.

Andy Murray and Kristy List. The class couple. They started dating in junior high.

They couldn't be in the house.

Please, please! Felicia prayed.

Don't let them be in the house.

chapter 11

"Come on!" Debbie yelled. She grabbed Felicia and pulled her up to the remains of the house.

Felicia grabbed a board and threw it behind her. She grabbed another one. Splinters bit into her palms. Nails tore at her skin. But Felicia didn't care. She had to find her friends.

"Andy! Kristy!" Felicia shouted until her throat felt raw.

She continued digging through the debris. Plaster dust filled her nose and lungs. She choked and coughed, her eyes burning.

"Noooo!" Debbie wailed.

Felicia ran over to her. Debbie turned away. She dropped to her knees and started to vomit.

Felicia stared down and saw an arm. Slender and freckled, with a friendship ring on one finger.

"Oh, Kristy!" Felicia cried. One of the support beams had cut off Kristy's arm. Felicia could see the white bone and the ragged layers of muscle.

Felicia knelt and slowly uncovered the rest of Kristy's body. She found Andy lying close beside his girlfriend.

I wouldn't have recognized him, Felicia thought. If I hadn't seen his car, I wouldn't have known this was Andy.

Bricks had crushed Andy's face. His nose and lips and eyelids scraped raw. Tears stung Felicia's eyes. *I did this,* she thought. *I killed them.*

Shadyside

Felicia shivered. She would never forget the dead, staring eyes of Andy and Kristy as long as she lived.

She pushed herself to walk faster. Unable to shake the feeling that someone watched her. Followed her from a distance.

She wanted to be home. Locked safe inside with Miss Quiz.

Almost dark, Felicia thought as she turned onto Fear Street. Faint yellow light gleamed in some windows. But most remained dark.

Dr. Jones's house came into view. Felicia took a quick glance behind her. The street still stood empty. Good.

She marched across the lawn and climbed the porch steps two at a time. I have to get inside. Now.

Felicia yanked the key from her pocket—and dropped it. Calm down, she ordered herself. No one is following you. You're home. You're okay.

She reached down and grabbed the key from the porch. A sliver of wood jabbed into her finger.

"Ouch!" Felicia exclaimed. She pulled the splinter out with her teeth.

Miss Quiz stood up at her spot on the living room windowsill. The cat gave a huge stretch.

Felicia tapped on the glass. "Hey, kitty," she called. She slid her key into the lock—and the front door swung open.

It was unlocked, Felicia realized.

I locked it this morning. I'm positive.

Felicia's heart skipped a beat. Is someone in there? A burglar?

Or the person who left me that note. The person who burned away my picture.

A tiny ripple of her power ran through her. No, she thought. I'm not letting it out. It's too dangerous.

Felicia stepped inside and paused. Miss Quiz ran up and rubbed against her legs, purring loudly. Miss Quiz isn't upset, she noticed. Maybe nobody came in, after all.

Cats aren't like dogs, Felicia warned herself. Miss Quiz wouldn't care if a stranger came into the house—as long as he left her alone.

Felicia moved into the foyer. She peered into the living room. Empty.

She took a deep breath and darted into the dining room. Empty.

Felicia snatched up the steel poker from the fireplace stand. It felt good in her hand. Heavy.

The doorway to the kitchen stood across the room.

Find the light switch and flick it on, she told herself. That's all you have to do.

She chanced a step forward—and stopped.

What was that?

Creak.

She heard the sound again.

Where is it coming from? Upstairs? Downstairs? Right behind her? She couldn't tell.

Felicia spun around. Nothing behind her.

Keep moving, she urged herself. She scurried to the kitchen doorway and ran her hands across the wall. Where is the light switch?

Got it. Felicia snapped the light on.

The kitchen stood empty too.

Next came Felicia's favorite room. Dr. Jones's den, where she liked to read and study.

And after that, I have two more floors upstairs and the basement to check, she thought grimly. If I don't have a heart attack first.

Felicia tightened her grip on the poker and crept into the hallway. Maybe I did forget to pull the front door all the way shut this morning, she thought.

But she knew she would never forget something like that.

The hallway narrowed as Felicia neared the den. Tall shelves overflowing with books towered over her on both sides. Felicia couldn't believe how many books Dr. Jones owned. It would take her a lifetime to make a dent in them.

She reached the doorway to the den and fumbled for the light switch.

A heavy hand came down on her shoulder.

"Get away from me!" Felicia screamed. She turned around fast and raised the poker high over her head.

Meow.

Miss Quiz leaped from Felicia's shoulder to the top bookshelf.

Felicia moaned. "Oh, Miss Quiz, you almost got your head whonked! What are you trying to do to me?"

"Meow," was Miss Quiz's only response.

"You *should* be sorry," Felicia muttered. She turned back to the den and flicked on the light.

What she saw made her stomach clench. A sharp acid taste flooded the back of her throat.

Someone has *been here.*

The contents of Dr. Jones's rolltop desk lay scattered on the floor. Along with pages torn from Felicia's schoolbooks. Her clothes. Her cassette tapes. Everything she owned.

Who did this? Who hates me so much?

Felicia picked up her favorite pullover shirt. Shredded. She couldn't even wear it around the house.

I can't stay here. I can't stay in this room. She turned—and uttered a low moan of terror.

Dripping red letters covered the wall.

Is that blood? Felicia thought.

She focused on the message, struggling to read the smeared letters.

Her heart pounded in her ears as she realized what the message said.

RUNAWAY! GET OUT NOW! I KNOW EVERYTHING!

chapter

12

Everything! That meant they knew about Andy and Kristy. They knew Felicia was a killer.

Felicia stepped up to the wall. She reached out and touched a drop of the glossy red liquid. She rubbed it between her fingers.

Not blood, she thought. Paint. And it's not quite dry.

Whoever did this hasn't been gone long.

Felicia quickly checked every floor of the house. Empty.

She thought so. It didn't make sense for someone to leave her that message—and then wait around for her to find it.

She hurried into the kitchen and filled a bucket with warm, soapy water. She grabbed as many sponges as she could find and headed back to the den.

Felicia set the bucket in front of the paint-smeared wall. She dunked a sponge into the warm water and attacked the huge red letters. She scrubbed until her shoulders ached. Until her arms trembled.

I'm not going to let you win, she thought. It's going to take a lot more than this to beat me.

Felicia hauled the bucket back to the sink and emptied it. She shuddered as she watched the red water splash onto the white enamel.

Felicia rung out the sponges and refilled the bucket. She dumped some food in Miss Quiz's bowl and gave the cat some fresh water. Then she grabbed the bucket and returned to the den.

She scrubbed until no trace of the red paint remained. Then she gathered up the professor's papers from the floor and arranged them neatly in the desk.

Felicia stretched her arms over her head until she could feel her muscles straining. Then she bent over and let her palms rest on the floor.

Her muscles felt tight. She took a deep breath and tried to relax deeper into her stretch. But she couldn't stop thinking about someone breaking in and going through all her things.

Felicia straightened up with a sigh. Now I have to get started on *my* stuff.

By the time she had the room back in order it was five in the morning. Only a couple of hours to sleep before school, she thought.

Felicia wished she could skip a day. But cutting

school was dangerous. She didn't want to give her teachers or the principal any reason to start asking questions about her parents. That could be dangerous.

"Are you okay?" Nick asked that evening.

"Huh?" Felicia asked, yawning.

"I said . . . are . . . you . . . oh . . . kay," Nick repeated. He sat across from her, chewing a Burger Basket Bellybuster—their biggest seller.

They had decided to spend their half-hour dinner break outside behind the restaurant. A small picnic table for employees sat near the Dumpster.

"I'm fine," she finally answered.

"You haven't touched your food."

Felicia groaned and pushed her meal aside. "If I eat any more deep-fried food, I'll hurl."

"What's going on?" he asked. "You look exhausted."

Felicia almost wished Zan were working that night. She didn't feel up to a heart-to-heart conversation with Nick.

"I haven't been sleeping," she answered.

"Nightmares?" he asked.

Her eyes narrowed. "What do you know about it?"

"Nothing," he replied. "But that's one reason why people don't sleep. Another is stress."

"You don't know anything, Nick," Felicia muttered. "Just forget about it."

"You're right," he agreed bitterly. "I *don't* know anything. Not one thing."

Felicia glared at him. He ignored it. He reached out and grasped her hand, squeezing it tight.

"Tell me what's wrong," he demanded.

"I'm a runaway," Felicia said simply.

Nick nodded. "I know. You told me that."

"Yeah, but it's not that simple."

"So confuse me."

"My parents are dead. My dad died about ten years ago." Felicia fought to keep her voice steady.

"What about your mom?"

"She died giving birth to me," Felicia replied.

Nick didn't say anything.

"I hated living with my Aunt Margaret," Felicia continued. "She meant well, I guess. And I love her. She's my family, you know? My father's sister. But we argued all the time."

"So," he replied cautiously. "That's why you left."

She nodded.

"That's cool, Felicia. I—"

"No, Nick," she interrupted. "No."

"What?"

"There's . . . there's more."

"More?"

"Much more." Felicia shifted uncomfortably. She had a hard time meeting Nick's gaze.

"It's okay," Nick assured her.

"I was part of something back there," she said. "Something at the local college that no one knew about."

Nick leaned forward. "What kind of thing?"

"Um, an experiment in their psych department. They were sort of . . . testing me."

"Testing you," Nick repeated. "For what?"

Felicia paused for a moment. She couldn't help grinning.

"What's so funny?"

"This is," she replied, laughing nervously. "I mean, it's so outrageous. I can't believe I'm sitting here about to tell you all this. You'll never believe it!"

Nick laughed with her. "Come on, Felicia. You're killing me here! What is it?"

Felicia took a deep breath. "They were mind experiments, Nick. But not the kind in any textbook."

"I don't get it," Nick replied.

I can't tell him, Felicia realized. I want to, but I can't. He'll think I'm some kind of freak.

"The doctors thought they could find out things about the brain or something," Felicia told him quickly. "I didn't really understand what they wanted. But for some reason I was the one they wanted to test."

Don't ask any questions, Felicia silently begged him.

"That doesn't make sense," Nick declared angrily. "Don't they need consent for that sort of thing?"

"They *got* consent—from Aunt Margaret. She thought it was good for me." Felicia sighed. She felt better now that her lie was in place and running smoothly.

"Anyway, I had to get out of there. The doctors wanted me at the lab almost all the time. I lost all my friends. I missed my father. I couldn't take it. I had to run."

"And now?"

"This," she replied, gesturing to the surroundings. "Shadyside. A new identity. A new life." She pulled his hand closer. "A new friend."

"Absolutely," Nick agreed with a smile. He leaned forward and kissed her on the lips.

Felicia blinked. "Nick!"

Nick shrugged. "It was my turn to kiss you."

A warm feeling rushed through her body. Finally she could be close to someone. Even if she couldn't tell him *everything*.

Nick leaned toward her again. His eyes focused on her lips.

Felicia tilted her head, ready for his kiss.

Bang! The back door to the restaurant flew open.

Felicia jerked away from Nick. She felt her face go hot.

Barry stuck his head out. "Back to work, drones!"

Thank goodness that wasn't Zan, Felicia thought. She tossed her trash in the Dumpster and hurried inside without waiting for Nick.

At ten, Barry locked the front doors. A few minutes later, someone knocked on the back door.

"I got it," Felicia called. She set her pile of dirty trays by the big sink and pulled open the door.

Zan stood there dressed all in black, from her boots to her leggings to her long sweater. Her eyes appeared even bluer than usual.

"You and Nick working alone tonight, huh?" Zan asked.

"Um, not really. Barry is here." Please don't let me blush, Felicia thought. She stepped back and Zan strolled through the door.

"Hey, Nick! Your chauffeur is here," she called. She grinned at Felicia.

Nick trotted into the back room. Zan grabbed him by the hand and tugged him toward the door. "Let's get out of here. I hate being in this place when I'm not working."

"See you tomorrow," Nick called over his shoulder. He caught Felicia's gaze and held it for a long moment. Then he was gone.

Felicia waited a few minutes to gather her things and punch out. She didn't want to watch Nick and Zan drive off together.

"You need a ride?" Barry asked, as she headed toward the back exit.

"No thanks. I'll walk. I need the exercise."

Barry nodded and saluted goodbye.

Felicia opened the back door and inhaled the chilly night air. She heard voices. Angry voices.

Nick and Zan.

Maybe I can leave without them seeing me, Felicia thought. I don't want to barge in on them in the middle of a fight.

She slipped past the Dumpster, staying close to the wall.

Then she heard something that stopped her cold.

"You watch yourself, Nick," Zan warned him. "I know the truth about Felicia. I know *everything!*"

chapter 13

Zan. Zan knows.

A chill shot through Felicia's body.

Is Zan the one who wants to hurt me? Did she steal my driver's license and paint that horrible message on Dr. Jones's wall?

Felicia hurried around the corner of the Burger Basket. She didn't want Zan to see her and realize that she had heard.

"Just stay away from her, okay?" she heard Zan yell, her voice high and shrill.

Felicia started to jog. She felt her power swelling inside her. No! she ordered herself. Don't let it out.

Felicia concentrated on the sound of her sneakers hitting the pavement. Stay calm. Stay calm. Stay calm. She repeated the words over and over in time with her footfalls.

She felt her power retreat. Maybe I'm finally learning to control it, Felicia thought.

She slowed to a walk, her thoughts returning to Zan. Even if Zan *did* take my license, all she would know is my real name and address. That wouldn't tell her much.

Except it had my Ridgely address, she thought. Maybe Zan wanted to find out something bad about me—to make sure Nick didn't get too interested.

Could Zan have retraced my steps back to Ridgely? Could she have found out about the house on the beach? About the way I killed Andy and Kristy?

Felicia doubted it. Hardly anyone in Ridgely knew about her powers. The police did—because they talked to Dr. Shanks and the others. But they wouldn't go around telling people she knocked down a building with her mind. That was top-secret stuff.

Felicia remembered how cold and angry Zan sounded when she told Nick to stay away from Felicia.

I won't know what to do until I find out if Zan discovered the truth, Felicia thought. I need to find out right away.

The next morning, Felicia stopped by Nick's locker. "Where's Zan?" she asked, trying to sound casual.

"I don't know," Nick replied. "I haven't seen her yet."

"Um, Nick?"

How am I supposed to ask this? she thought. Nick and Zan's problems were none of her business.

Unless my name comes up in their fights, she corrected herself.

"What?" Nick slammed his locker door shut.

"Last night I heard you and Zan arguing outside the Burger Basket."

Nick rolled his eyes and groaned.

"I'm sorry," Felicia told him. "I didn't mean to eavesdrop, but you were pretty loud."

"Yeah, I know." Nick shrugged. "Zan has a real jealous streak."

"Really?" Felicia wished she could be more honest with Nick. But she couldn't risk it.

"What did you hear us say?" Nick asked.

"Not much," Felicia replied. "I walked away. But I did hear her say something like 'I know the truth about Felicia.'"

"Yeah." Nick snorted. "Zan seems to think that the two of us are getting too close."

Felicia paused. "We are?"

"I don't think so," Nick complained. "Zan gets angry and says things she doesn't mean. She likes you, Felicia. She really does. But she's just jealous sometimes."

"So, what does she *know* about me?" Felicia asked, careful to keep her tone even.

"Nothing," Nick replied. "But in her mind, she knows all about the 'relationship' we've been having. I keep telling her we're just friends. . . ."

Friends who keep wanting to kiss each other, Felicia silently added. But she felt relieved. Zan didn't know any more about Felicia's past than Nick did.

Felicia felt embarrassed that she assumed the worst about Zan. But it had sounded as if she knew a horrible secret about Felicia.

"Felicia?" Nick asked.

"Yeah?"

"This whole thing with Zan. I smoothed it over last night. She's not angry or anything. But can I ask a favor?"

"Sure."

"I'm sorry if last night upset you. But I don't want you to blame Zan for any of what you heard." He gazed at her intently.

"I'm not really upset," Felicia said quickly.

"That's good . . . Zan's been through a hard time. It was pretty bad. She doesn't mean to be mean. Try to be extra nice to her, okay? For me?"

"Am I allowed to ask what kind of a hard time she's had?"

Nick shook his head. "Actually, no."

"Hey, come on, Nick," Felicia pressed. "I trusted you with a lot last night. Don't you think you can trust me now?"

"Of course I trust you," Nick insisted. "And you trust me, right?"

"I just said I did."

"Well, so does Zan," Nick shot back. "If she wants you to know, she'll tell you herself."

"I'm sorry, Nick. You're right," Felicia told him.

"That's okay. You're a good friend," Nick told her.

Felicia managed a stiff smile. She wished things

could be different. She wished she and Nick could be more than friends.

But he had a girlfriend. A jealous girlfriend. And Felicia had too many secrets.

Friday at last, Felicia thought a few days later. And she had the night off. She could use it. It had been a rough week.

She opened the door to her locker and pulled out the books she needed before lunch. After school she promised herself she would go straight home and kick back. Maybe even take a nap. She still hadn't caught up on the sleep she lost on her all-night cleaning spree.

"Felicia?"

Felicia shut her locker and turned around. Zan stood watching her. "Hey, how's it going?" Felicia felt weird talking to Zan now that she knew how Zan felt about her and Nick.

"Great!" Zan answered. "I've been wanting to talk to you all week, but I didn't get a chance. Do you have a minute?"

"Sure," Felicia replied. "But not much more than that. My first class is on the other side of school."

"I wanted to find out if you're doing anything tonight." Zan pulled a red scrunchie out of her shiny black hair, smoothed down her ponytail, and put it back in again.

"Um, nothing much." I hope she doesn't want to trade shifts, Felicia thought. I'm beat.

"Want to come over and spend the night at my house? We can rent some movies or something."

Felicia wanted to say no. An evening with Zan didn't sound exactly relaxing—even though Zan seemed perfectly friendly. But she remembered what Nick said about being nice to Zan.

"Sounds good," Felicia answered. "We never get a chance to talk—except over the deep fryer."

Zan grinned. "It will be fun," she assured Felicia. "Come any time after dinner." She waved and walked off down the hall.

Maybe it *will* be fun, Felicia thought as she headed for class. I haven't hung out with another girl for so long.

Not since Debbie.

Felicia swallowed down the lump in her throat. She missed Debbie. Missed their sleepovers, talking half the night, eating junk food.

But now I have Zan, she told herself. Now I have new friends.

Felicia arrived at Zan's about a quarter after eight. Zan's house was huge. Even bigger than the professor's.

She liked the dark green trim around the windows. And the balconies overlooking the manicured landscape of evergreen shrubs and tall, sprawling oak trees.

The tall wrought-iron gate swung smoothly on its hinges when Felicia pushed it open. Each bar of the fence ended in a sharp point at least an inch thick. Wow, Felicia thought, no one's getting over this fence without a fight!

She hurried up the walkway and rang the bell.

"Great house," Felicia said when Zan opened the door.

"Thanks," Zan replied. "My parents are fanatics about it. They work on it constantly."

Zan led the way inside and Felicia met her parents for all of fifteen seconds. They were on their way out, and wouldn't be home until late. Good, Felicia thought. Now she wouldn't have to come up with answers about her parents or where she lived before.

"Let's go up to my room," Zan said when they left. She climbed up a long flight of stairs, Felicia right behind her. Zan pulled open the first door on the left.

Whoa, Felicia thought. Her room is amazing! A massive king-sized bed sat against one wall with a matching desk and dresser across from it. A pair of French doors led out onto one of the balconies Felicia had seen on her way in.

"Zan, this is without a doubt the coolest room I've ever seen."

"Thanks." Zan popped in a CD and cranked up the volume.

"Do you have any brothers or sisters?" Felicia asked.

"Nope," Zan replied. "It's just me. And I like it that way. What about you?"

"Me neither." Felicia pulled a video from her backpack and tossed it to Zan. A copy of *The Birds* she found at Dr. Jones's. "It's Hitchcock," Felicia told Zan. "Have you ever seen it?"

"Is it any good?"

"Awesome," Felicia promised. "It'll scare you to *death.*"

"Cool. I'm all ready. I made popcorn and everything. I even got those chocolate-covered raisins." Zan popped the tape in and shut off the music.

This is much better than staying at home with only Miss Quiz for company, Felicia thought.

"If I eat any more popcorn, I'm going to blow up," Felicia moaned when the movie ended.

"I can't believe you put away two bowls," Zan replied.

"It's weird. When a movie comes on, I pig out. I can't help it."

"You want some more soda?" Zan asked. "I'm going."

"Sure."

"I'll nuke some cheese and salsa, too," Zan said. "Mom told me to make sure I gave you some *real* food."

"I'm going to burst!"

"Be back in five."

Felicia stood up and wandered over to Zan's bookshelf. A few bestsellers, some classics, some ancient children's books. Then she noticed Zan's Shadyside High yearbooks.

She pulled down the one from Zan's sophomore year and plopped onto the bed. Now I get to see how dumb everyone looked back then, she thought.

She flipped through, glancing at the pictures. She spotted one of Nick, and couldn't help giggling. He had such a round baby face. And he was definitely having a bad hair day.

I don't need Zan to walk in and find me staring at a picture of her boyfriend, Felicia thought. Especially now that everything is okay between us again.

Felicia turned the page. It felt thicker than the other pages. It's two stuck together, she realized. She carefully peeled the pages apart.

A picture of Zan stared up at her.

But who is she with? Felicia wondered. The other half of the photo had been inked out with a brown marker. She could only read half the caption:

THE COUPLE MOST

Felicia listened for a moment. Was Zan coming back upstairs? No.

I'm being a total snoop, she thought. But I'm not really hurting anything.

Felicia wet the tip of her index finger and gently rubbed at the ink. It felt crusty.

She rubbed harder. The ink started coming off on her fingertip, but she still couldn't see underneath. She couldn't see who Zan was with.

Felicia shot a glance at the door. I should put this away, she thought. Zan obviously doesn't want anyone to look at this picture.

But she felt so curious. She couldn't stop now. Felicia spit on the page and spread the saliva around.

Then she smelled it.

A metallic smell, like a handful of pennies.

Felicia knew that odor. She smelled it the day she

uncovered the torn bodies of Andy Murray and Kristy List.

She raised her fingers in front of her eyes. A glistening red substance covered them. Not brown—red.

Felicia's breath caught in her chest.

This stuff isn't ink, she thought. It's . . . it's . . . Blood.

chapter

14

*F*elicia heard footsteps on the stairs.

Zan!

She slammed the yearbook shut and shoved it back into the bookshelf where she found it.

Uh-oh! Zan will see the blood on my fingers. Felicia darted to the bedroom door. She needed to find a bathroom and wash up. Felicia jerked open the door.

Zan stood there with a big plate of nachos and two Diet Cokes balanced in her hands. "Thanks," Zan said. "I think I tried to carry too much stuff at once."

Felicia forced herself to smile. She balled up her bloodstained hand into a fist at her side.

"I need to use the bathroom," Felicia said.

Zan set down the nachos and popped open a can of soda. "It's right next door."

"Be right back," Felicia replied. She hurried into the bathroom and locked the door. Whew! She let out a big sigh. *What would Zan have done if she caught me staring at that photo?* Felicia wondered.

She turned on the hot water and let it run for a moment. Then she squirted some liquid soap on her fingers and scrubbed them until they felt raw.

How did Zan get enough blood to cover half that picture? Did she cut her finger and let it bleed on the page or something? Felicia shuddered.

Definitely a bad *breakup*, she thought. She shut off the hot water and turned on the cold. She splashed her face a few times, then dried it with a pale peach guest towel.

She gazed around the bathroom. No blood left in the sink. Nothing on the towels. *Cool.*

She returned to Zan's room. "Hurry up," Zan urged. "This stuff's getting cold."

Felicia picked up a chip covered in gooey cheese and salsa. Her stomach lurched. She kept remembering that metallic blood smell.

You have to eat at least a few, Felicia told herself. *Zan will think it's weird if you don't.* She popped the chip in her mouth. Warm goo ran down her chin. *Yuck!*

"So," Felicia asked casually. "How long have you and Nick been going together?"

"Since freshman year," Zan replied.

"Wow, that's a long time," Felicia commented. *She's lying!* Felicia thought. *I know they haven't* been together that long. The part of the yearbook caption she could read said "the couple most." So unless Zan and Nick had a big fight—and then made up—Nick couldn't be the other half of the couple in the picture.

"Yeah, I know. We fight and everything, but I really can't get along without him."

"That is so great," Felicia said with genuine envy. "I hope I meet someone as nice as Nick."

"There are other guys at Shadyside High," Zan commented. "You have to get out more, that's all."

"That's for sure," Felicia agreed. "I sure won't meet them at the Burger Basket drive-thru window."

"Oh, I don't know. That guy in the big four-by-four the other night was a real winner!" Zan said sarcastically.

"I came this close, *this* close to asking him out, I swear!" Felicia said, rolling her eyes.

"He was cute!" Zan insisted. "Haven't you ever wondered what it would be like to date a guy like that?"

"Fat, dark, and sweaty? Pass," Felicia answered. "So what kind of music do you have?"

Zan gestured to her rack of compact discs. "Pick one."

Felicia crawled over to the stereo and scanned the titles. She couldn't stop thinking about that yearbook picture. What happened to make Zan cover the guy's photo in blood?

It had to be bad. Maybe something to do with the hard time Zan had been through.

What happened to her? Felicia wondered. What is Zan's big secret?

Felicia wandered through the rows of books in the school library on Monday morning. I shouldn't be doing this, she thought. I should be searching for the books I need for my history paper.

But she had something else in mind. She wanted to find the old school yearbooks. She wanted to study the picture she found at Zan's last week. See if she could figure out why Zan had smeared blood over the guy's picture.

There they are. Felicia spotted the Shadyside yearbook collection along the back wall. She scanned the spines for the year she wanted.

Yes! Felicia pulled out the book from Zan's sophomore year. She flipped through until she hit the page she wanted. This time she found no blood. No pages stuck together. Only the musty smell of aging paper.

And a portrait of Zan arm in arm with a handsome blond-haired guy. Felicia read the complete caption:

ALEXANDRIA McCONNELL AND DOUG GAYNOR, THE COUPLE MOST LIKELY TO LAST FOREVER.

Doug Gaynor? she thought. I was right. Zan and Nick *haven't* been together since freshman year!

Doug Gaynor. She didn't recognize his face . . . but the name sounded familiar. He wasn't in any of her classes. Where did she hear of him?

A chill flooded Felicia.

Now she remembered. She remembered exactly how she knew that name.

Felicia slammed the yearbook shut. Then she ran from the library without signing out. She didn't stop until she reached the second floor. A small wooden bench stood halfway down the hall. Felicia strode over to it, her heart hammering in her chest.

She raised her eyes to the brass plaque over the bench.

It read: *In Memory of Douglas Gaynor.*

Her heart pounded harder. It felt as if it might explode.

He's dead, she thought.

Zan's old boyfriend is dead!

chapter

15

"So, Zan said you two had a good time Friday," Nick commented. Felicia and he wandered over to the school parking lot. They both had to be at the Burger Basket in fifteen minutes. Zan's shift didn't start for another few hours.

"Yeah," Felicia mumbled as she climbed into Nick's car. She checked over her shoulder as he got in and started the engine. She glanced back again as he pulled into the street.

She kept hoping she would catch someone following her. At least then she would know who to be afraid of.

Nick checked the rearview mirror. "What are you looking for?" he asked.

"I'm always a little nervous that someone is watching me," she admitted.

Nick jerked his head toward her. "Why?" he demanded.

Should I give him the long answer or the short answer? Felicia wondered. She decided to start with the short one.

"Well, since I ran away, I've become sort of a con artist." That sounds so bad, Felicia thought. She hoped Nick would be able to understand.

"What do you mean?"

"Well . . . you know that house on Fear Street where I told you I live?"

"Yeah?"

"I sort of stole it."

"I don't get it. How do you steal a house?" Nick frowned at her.

"The house belongs to some guy named Dr. Jones. He teaches at the college. The day I got to town I overheard this guy say he was supposed to watch the place and take care of Dr. Jones's cat while he's on leave."

"Let me guess," Nick said. "You talked this guy into giving you the job."

Nick didn't sound upset or anything. Good. "I can be very charming," Felicia informed him. She smiled. "And I told him my father knew Dr. Jones."

Nick snorted. "I can guess the rest," he said. "Not only have you been taking care of the cat, you've been taking care of the fridge, the TV, and the sofa, too."

"You got it."

"So what?" Nick shrugged. "You did what you

had to do. You're not hurting anything. I don't know what happens when Dr. Jones gets back, but until then, why not?"

"Thanks. But that's not the real reason I'm afraid someone is following me." Felicia admitted.

"So?" Nick finally asked. "What is?"

"I think someone from my hometown followed me here."

"Really?"

"Either that, or someone from Shadyside knows about my past. It's one or the other, and I'm trying like crazy to find out which."

"How do you know?" Nick asked. He turned into the Burger Basket lot and parked the car. "Did something happen?"

Felicia nodded. It's now or never, she thought. Go for it.

She told Nick all about the burned note in her locker and the red words sprawled on Dr. Jones's walls that same night.

"If you think I blabbed to anybody all the things you told me, you're very, very wrong," he said firmly.

"I didn't say you did, Nick," Felicia replied. "But someone knows. And I'm scared."

Nick put his hand over hers and squeezed. Felicia slid across the seat. She wrapped her arms around him and buried her face in his shirt.

He held her tight. His flannel shirt felt warm under her cheek.

I could stay right here forever, Felicia thought. It had been too long since someone held her. Too long since someone cared about her.

"You don't have to be afraid," he whispered. She could feel his breath against her hair. "I'm here for you no matter what."

Felicia lifted her head and stared into his eyes. "Promise?"

"No matter what," he repeated.

Then they kissed.

It felt so right. Then Nick jerked away.

"No," Nick muttered. "No, I can't do this."

Felicia slid away from him. She rolled down the window and stared into the parking lot. The air felt cold against her face. Then she turned back to him. "What happened?"

"I love Zan," Nick said. He stared down at the steering wheel.

"I don't believe you." Felicia could hardly believe she said that out loud. But it was true. She just didn't believe he loved Zan. "I think you're afraid to break up with her."

"She needs me," he mumbled. "She wouldn't be able to take it."

"She's stronger than you think," Felicia insisted. "You shouldn't stay with her out of fear."

"You don't know anything about it," he shot back, his voice suddenly harsh and cold. "So drop it, okay?"

"Okay. After I ask you one more question." I hope he doesn't hate me for this, Felicia thought. She took a deep breath. "Does this have anything to do with Doug Gaynor?"

Nick swallowed hard. "What about him?" he whispered.

"You tell me."

"You really want to know?" he asked defiantly. "You think you can take it?"

"Yes!"

"Zan killed him."

chapter

16

"What?" Felicia gasped.

"It was an accident!" Nick cried. "Don't look at me that way. It was an accident!"

"What do you mean?" Felicia demanded. "Either she killed him or she didn't."

"She didn't mean to," Nick replied. "I know she didn't."

"What happened?"

"It's a long story."

"Give me a break, Nick," Felicia said angrily. "First you tell me she killed him. Now you're saying it was an accident. You owe me an explanation."

Nick sighed. "Doug died a couple of years ago. Zan didn't come to school for a long time. She had shrinks and tutors, and more shrinks. Her parents have some bucks, you know? Anyway, we started going out about six months ago."

"But what really happened to Doug?" Felicia pressed.

"I'm getting to that," Nick snapped. "Zan and Doug started going together in seventh grade. That's five years ago, Felicia. Man, I didn't go on my first date until sophomore year! Everyone thought Zan and Doug were the real thing. But then Doug got bored or something."

"He went out with someone behind her back?" Felicia asked.

"I don't really know for sure," Nick replied. "No one does. He went on one date with a girl named Kathleen Clarke. Her family left town a long time ago. But no one is sure if Doug actually broke up with Zan first."

Felicia nodded.

"It doesn't matter which way it happened," he continued. "The bottom line is that Zan found out."

"And she freaked," Felicia said.

"Yeah. You could say that. Doug came to see her the next night. I think he felt bad and wanted to apologize to Zan. He seemed like a cool guy, you know? Not the kind that ran around on his girlfriend. Anyway, they were talking on Zan's balcony. You know the one I mean?"

"Yeah, I saw it," Felicia replied.

"They started to argue about Kathleen, I guess. Zan went ballistic. She started hitting Doug. He tried to push her away—and she whacked her head against one of the French doors. That made her furious. She pushed back."

Nick paused. "Then Doug lost his balance," he said quietly.

"He fell," Felicia concluded. She felt her stomach twist into a knot.

"Yeah . . . but that's not what killed him."

Felicia felt confused. "Huh? What killed him?"

Nick swallowed hard. "You know that wrought-iron fence that surrounds the property?"

Felicia covered her mouth. She could picture the fence . . . iron, with thick, sharp points at the top.

"Four spikes sliced through Doug's back," Nick whispered. "Another slashed through his left arm." He cleared his throat. "The TV news said that he didn't die right away. It took some time."

Felicia began to shake. What a horrible way to die.

And Zan was responsible. Felicia could almost see Zan standing above Doug's impaled body. Staring down at him as he quivered on the spikes. As blood poured from his chest. As he gurgled a cry for help through mouthfuls of blood.

Felicia wrapped her arms around herself. Doug Gaynor probably saw the spikes sticking out of his chest. Knew Zan stood above him. Knew he was going to die.

How horrible. How horrible for Zan. Felicia knew how it felt to live knowing you killed another person. It didn't help to tell yourself it was an accident. It didn't help to tell yourself you didn't mean to do it.

"Now you understand why I can't break up with

her," Nick said softly. "I can't put her through that again. Not now. She's not strong enough. She hasn't even been back in school a whole year."

The yearbook photo flashed into Felicia's mind. She remembered how every inch of Doug's half of the photo had been covered with blood.

Carefully covered. Neatly covered. Not even a drop on Zan's half.

She blotted Doug out of her life, Felicia thought. She lied to me about how long she's been dating Nick.

Is she that cold? That cruel? Could Zan have intended to kill him?

If she did, if Zan did kill Doug . . . what would she do to me? Felicia thought.

She rubbed her arms. Her whole body felt chilled.

I thought those messages were from someone who knew my past. Someone who wanted to make me pay for what happened to Kristy and Andy.

She drew in a shaky breath. But I was wrong. Zan must have sent me the note. She must have trashed Dr. Jones's den.

Zan doesn't care about my past. All she cares about is Nick. She must have been trying to scare me away from him.

But I didn't go.

Felicia grabbed Nick's arm. "Zan must be the one who left me those threatening notes. She felt jealous of me from the beginning. Remember? She pointed that butcher knife at me and told me to stay away from you. I thought it was a sick joke."

Felicia spoke faster and faster, her fingernails

digging into Nick's arm. "But Zan was serious. She's going to come after me now. She's going to kill me the way she killed Doug!"

"Stop! Zan didn't kill Doug. I told you it was an accident," Nick cried. "First you think some *scientists* are trying to track you down. Now you think Zan is trying to kill you. Get a grip on reality, okay?"

Felicia released his arm. "Fine," she said. "But someone put that note in my locker. Someone painted that threat on the wall. If Zan didn't do it, who did?"

"I never saw any of that stuff," Nick muttered.

Felicia felt tears sting her eyes. She blinked them away. If Nick didn't believe her, fine. She was used to being alone. She didn't need him.

"It's time for work," she said. "Barry's going to be out here in thirty seconds screaming at us."

"You have to promise me something first."

"What?" Felicia grabbed the door handle. She wanted to get away from him—now.

"You can never let Zan know I told you all this."

"I promise," she replied evenly. She wasn't going to let Nick see how much he hurt her. "Zan will never find out."

"Find out what?" came Zan's angry voice.

chapter
17

"Zan!" Nick choked out. "What are *you* doing here?"

Zan leaned down and stared at them through Felicia's window. "Barry asked me to come early," she replied icily. "I guess I got here just in time."

Felicia tried to smile. "Hey, how's it going?" she asked, hoping Zan hadn't heard too much.

Zan shook her head. "I asked you a question. Zan won't find out *what?*"

Felicia glanced at Nick. He appeared clueless. Think fast, she told herself.

"Nick asked my advice about something," Felicia blurted out. I hope he follows my lead, she thought.

"Advice?" Zan sneered. "What advice could you possibly give him?"

"I wanted to take you out someplace special," Nick said. "I thought Felicia might have some good ideas."

"What?" Zan snapped, as if it was the dumbest thing she'd ever heard.

"We haven't gone out in a long time. We're both always at school or work," Nick explained. "I wanted to plan something nice."

Zan didn't say anything.

Is she buying it? Felicia wondered.

"Felicia even agreed to take one of your shifts so we could have the same night off," Nick added.

"Surprise!" Felicia cried.

She stared up at Zan. Have you been threatening me? she thought. Are you the one?

"That's it?" Zan finally said. *"That's* the big secret I could never hear?"

"What did you think it was?" Nick asked irritably.

"I'm sorry." Zan bit her lip. "I know I have to stop being so suspicious."

"Definitely," Felicia replied. "We're friends, right?"

Felicia climbed out of the car.

Zan hurried over to Nick and wrapped her arms around his waist. "Why don't we all celebrate by going inside and slinging some grease at the customers?" he asked.

"Sounds like a good plan," Felicia said.

Nick and Zan led the way to the back door of the Burger Basket. As they stepped inside, Nick glanced over his shoulder. "Thank you," he mouthed to Felicia.

Felicia nodded. I guess we're all friends again, she thought. Until I find out the truth about Zan.

"Does *this* burger look like the one in the picture?" a customer demanded. "I don't *think* so!"

Felicia sighed. Is there a full moon tonight, or what? she thought. Everyone who comes in here tonight has an attitude.

She gave the customer a fresh burger. Then she poured herself a big Diet Coke. "I'm taking a break," Felicia mumbled to Zan as she headed toward the back room. "Tell Barry for me, okay?"

"Oh, Felicia, wait!" Zan called over her shoulder as she dumped a new batch of fries into the warmer. "Before you do, could you change the lightbulb in the storage room? It's burned out."

Felicia tried not to sigh. "No problem."

"Thanks," Zan replied.

Felicia trudged back to the storage room. She fumbled around for a new lightbulb. Then she grabbed the metal ladder and hauled it into the middle of the room.

She heard a sloshing sound as she walked. Then she felt water soaking into her shoes. Someone had spilled the mop bucket and—as usual—didn't mop it up. "Great," Felicia muttered. "Who's the slob?"

I'm not doing it, she thought. Let them clean up their own mess. She unfolded the stepladder, made sure it felt steady, and climbed up, cradling the new lightbulb in one hand.

Felicia stood on tiptoe on the ladder, reaching up

for the old bulb. She could barely see it in the darkness.

Her hand bumped against the bulb. It swung back and forth on its long wire. Felicia grabbed for it.

A bright spark blasted out from the wire. Felicia jumped and dropped the new bulb. It hit the wet floor and shattered.

The harsh scent of burning plastic filled her nose. She heard a humming sound above her. A soft crackle.

Felicia took a step down. Something shiny caught her eye. Something coppery.

The wire is frayed, she realized. That's why the old bulb is out, because someone cut open the wire.

A shot of panic went through her.

"I'm out of here," she whispered.

She jumped off the ladder, shoes landing with a splash and crunch in the water and broken glass. She backed away, her knees weak. Water on the floor . . . a frayed wire . . . a metal stepladder.

I could have been fried!

Felicia turned and rushed to the circuit breakers near the back door. She had to cut off the electricity before someone got hurt.

She opened the door to the power box and studied the labels. A flash of movement caught her eye. She jerked her head and saw Barry shove through the storage room door.

"Why is it so dark in here?" he grumbled.

He reached for the chain to switch on the light. *"Barry—no!"* Felicia screamed.

chapter

18

Barry missed the chain and grabbed the cut wire.

A flash of bright white light exploded into the room. The air sizzled.

Barry shrieked in agony. The charge blasted him across the room off the ladder—the wire still clutched in his hand.

He slammed into the metal supply shelves. The wire sparked when it touched the metal.

Felicia stared at his limp body. At the wisps of smoke sizzling off his hair and clothes.

"What happened?" she heard Nick call.

Felicia jerked into action. She reached for the main power switch. Sparks crackled from the circuit box. She yanked her hand away.

"Get everyone out of here—now!" Felicia

yelled. "The wiring is frying. The whole place will be on fire in a minute." She ran back behind the counter. *"Go!"* she shouted to the blond woman at the front of the line.

Too late.

Felicia froze. She couldn't run. Couldn't move. The hair on her arms stood straight up.

Power shot through the restaurant's wiring.

The fluorescent lights shattered. Razor-sharp slivers flew.

Flames shot out from the electrical outlet.

The cash register drawers sprang open. Dollar bills and change spewed out.

Zan hit the floor, covering her head with her arms.

All Felicia could do was stare. Her eyes followed the destruction from light to light, all across the restaurant.

Then her gaze locked on the microwaves—and on Nick, standing right in front of them.

"Nick! Get away!" Felicia screamed.

Nick dropped to his knees.

The electricity hit the microwaves. They exploded. Food, burning plastic, and glass rained down on Nick.

The heating lamps. They are going next, Felicia realized. Before she could shout a warning, they erupted.

White-hot sparks showered the deep fryers.

The oil burst into towers of flame.

Someone uttered a low moan of terror.

A chunk of the ceiling caved in and blocked the front entrance with a wall of fire.

Adrenaline pumped through Felicia's body. Get out! she ordered herself. Get out now!

Barry! she thought. I can't leave him back there. He might only be unconscious. He'll burn to death.

She ran to the storage room, her feet sliding on the wet floor. Barry lay sprawled on his back on the floor. He hadn't moved.

Felicia knelt beside him and slipped her arm under his back. She struggled to pull him to his feet.

He's too heavy!

Felicia lowered him to the floor. She sucked in a deep breath. Thick smoke burned her throat. Filled her lungs. She choked.

A figure moved through the smoke toward her. Nick!

"Are you okay?" he yelled.

"Help me get Barry out of here," she cried. "He's too heavy for me."

"Pull him!" Nick bellowed. "Grab him by the feet. Pull him out the back door! I'm going to try and make it up front. People need help getting out."

Felicia picked up Barry's feet. No shoes, she noticed. *He was blown right out of them!*

Felicia pulled with all of her strength. Barry's body started to slide across the tile floor.

Only a few more steps to the door, she thought. Pull! Pull! Pull! Smoke swirled into her eyes. Each breath seemed to contain more smoke—and less air.

Bright colors danced in front of Felicia's eyes. She felt dizzy. She swayed on her feet.

Can't do it, she thought. Can't.

Then she felt the metal bolt hit her back. The one across the middle of the back door.

Relief flooded Felicia. She slammed her weight against it. The door flew open. Her momentum carried her outside. She dragged Barry out with her.

She stumbled and fell to the cement near the Dumpster. She panted, frantic to fill her lungs with air.

With each breath she felt stronger. I made it! I'm alive!

But Nick is still inside.

Felicia stared at the wall of flames now blocking the back door. Soaring higher with the fresh supply of oxygen from the open door.

I'll never make it back there. It's impossible.

Then an idea hit her.

"I have to go, Barry," she said grimly, even though she knew he couldn't hear her. "Please don't die."

She shoved herself to her feet and sprinted around the front corner of the Burger Basket. Smoke blocked every window. Flames broke through the ceiling in several places.

Felicia knew everyone in that restaurant would live or die depending on her actions. She could not fail.

Felicia took a deep breath and ran to the side door that led directly into the dining area. The flesh of her fingers sizzled when she grabbed the handle, but she ignored the pain and plunged inside.

Flames poured from the kitchen across the ceiling. Huge flakes of red-hot ash floated in the air.

Remember the old beach house, she told herself. You can do this.

This time she *wanted* her power. She wanted it *all*.

Felicia stood perfectly still. Heat seared her skin. Smoke burned her eyes, rushing into her lungs with each breath.

She closed her eyes and formed a picture of the fire in her mind.

Felicia pushed against its force with all her might, feeling the power rage through her system.

And in her mind, the flames began to retreat. The smoke cleared. The air felt cooler.

"What's happening?" came a voice from the dining area. "What is she doing?"

"Who cares!" another screamed. "Let me out!"

Felicia opened her eyes. She took a step forward—commanding her power to push the flames back. "Zan! Nick!" Felicia screamed. "Nick! Answer me!"

A tall man shoved his way past her. "Get out of here! Are you nuts?"

She pushed even harder. The flames shuddered and retreated.

Felicia reached the front counter. The plastic countertop bubbled. Yellow smoke rose from it.

Felicia gagged. *No,* she raged. *Don't let go now!*

She shut her eyes and forced the flames back.

Through the smoke she spotted a group of people staggering toward her. She reached deeper into her power—and aimed it at them. She willed them forward. And pushed the flames back.

The fire pushed against her with a raging force. Felicia knew her power couldn't hold it much longer.

"Run!" she screamed. "Run! Get out of here! Go!"

Nick and two other teenagers stumbled through the smoke. "What about you?" Nick yelled.

"Just go!" she ordered. She had so little strength left.

"I'm not leaving without you," Nick croaked. He shoved the other kids toward the door.

"No, Nick," she pleaded. "You don't understand! *You have to go first!"*

She didn't have time to argue. The flames moved in.

I can't hold them back. Too strong. Too hot.

The flames rushed forward. Felicia and Nick threw themselves face down on the floor. She watched in horror as the fire consumed the door the others had gone through.

"Our last exit—it's blocked," Nick cried.

Anger flooded Felicia. She would *not* let this happen! *"I'm not dying like this!"* she screamed. Pain ripped through her lungs. The power crackled through her mind.

She spotted one of the dining room chairs—and threw every ounce of her remaining power at it. It flew into the air and smashed through one of the front windows.

"Go!" she barked.

Nick shoved himself to his feet and stumbled to

the window. He dragged Felicia with him, his hands clamped tightly onto her arm.

Felicia felt the power leave her, pouring out of her in a rush.

Her legs collapsed. She crumpled to the floor. Exhausted. All her energy gone.

The flames rose up around her.

This is it, she thought helplessly. *This is what it feels like to die.*

chapter

19

*F*elicia struggled to open her eyes—and saw Nick's face.

"Felicia?" he whispered gently. "You okay?"

She smiled. I'm alive! We both are!

"Hi," she croaked.

Nick helped her sit up. She blinked away the grit in her eyes and stared around her. Firefighters sprayed water over the wreckage of the Burger Basket.

"How long was I out?" she asked.

"You were in and out for about fifteen minutes," Nick replied.

"The restaurant went down in fifteen minutes?"

Nick shrugged. "Most of it was gone by the time we got out. It didn't take much more."

"Wow."

Nick shook his head. "What do you think caused it? All I know is everything started exploding."

"A short circuit," Felicia said, remembering. "Oh no! Barry!"

"He's okay," Nick replied calmly. "He got a good wallop. But he's got a thick skull. The ambulance took him away already." Nick smiled at her. "You saved him, Felicia. And what you did after that . . . you saved us all."

Felicia didn't know what to say.

"What *did* you do in there?" he asked.

Felicia gazed into his eyes. "Please don't ask me that," she whispered.

Nick didn't protest. He simply met her stare. Accepting her plea. For now. Felicia didn't want to think about what would happen later.

What could she possibly tell him? *I threw my mind at the fire and it backed off.*

"There!" a voice called from across the busy parking lot. "That's her! She's the one who saved everybody."

At least a dozen reporters headed toward Felicia, spotlights and cameras bouncing.

"Oh, Nick, you have to get me out of here!" she gasped.

"Why?" he asked. "Don't you want to be a hero on TV?"

"No! No one can know who I am! The police will find me! I have to get out of here."

Nick reached in his pocket and handed her his keys. "Take my car. Run for it. Go back to your place until everything quiets down. Call me later."

Felicia grabbed the keys. The plastic Shadyside

High keychain was mangled and bent—and still warm.

That's how hot the fire was, she thought with a shudder. It melted the plastic in Nick's pocket!

"Run!" Nick prodded. "I'll try to block them."

"Thanks, Nick."

"Just *go*," he urged.

Felicia still felt weak and dazed. But she managed to weave her way through the bustling firefighters and into the crowd of onlookers.

The reporters reached Nick. "She doesn't want to talk to anyone!" Felicia heard him shout.

"Who is she?" someone called.

"Do you know her? What's her name? Where does she live?" another demanded.

Felicia caught another piece of conversation from behind her. "Of course I'm sure!" one of the customers insisted. "The flames backed away from her! Don't give me that! I'm telling you *exactly* what I saw!"

Oh no, Felicia thought. That guy's telling them everything! If word of what she did to save those people hit the papers, the Ridgely police would know where she was!

Felicia walked as fast as she could. But she felt dizzy and exhausted. Nick's car seemed miles away. But at last she reached it.

"Why didn't you just die?" a voice demanded. A female voice she barely recognized. Full of anger.

Felicia turned.

Zan. Her face covered with soot. Her Burger Basket uniform stained with sweat and grime. Her blue eyes burning bright and hateful.

"What?" Felicia gasped.

"You were supposed to die!" Zan screamed. "All you had to do was change a stupid lightbulb!"

Zan ran straight at Felicia, slamming into her before Felicia could move. They both crashed onto the sidewalk.

Felicia's head smacked the cement. Pain exploded behind her eyes.

Zan rolled on top of Felicia and clamped her hands around her throat.

She wants to kill me, Felicia realized. She tried to *electrocute* me.

Felicia reached down inside her, searching for the power to hurl Zan away. But she felt empty. She could barely lift her arms to struggle.

Zan bent close to Felicia, her face locked in an expression of fury. "You saved Nick," she whispered. "But that doesn't mean he belongs to you now. That doesn't mean you can take him from me."

Zan's fingers dug deeper into Felicia's throat. "You'll never go near Nick again."

Colors spun in Felicia's eyes. Her arms flopped at her sides.

She wheezed, struggling for air.

Zan's grip tightened.

chapter

20

"**Y**ou're supposed to die!" Zan wailed. "Why won't you die?"

Felicia choked, struggled to suck in some air.

"Stop it, Zan!" Felicia heard someone yell. The voice sounded far away. "Stop it! You're killing her!"

The hands lifted from her throat, and Felicia's lungs filled with cool, life-giving air. She rolled onto her side, concentrating on taking long, slow breaths.

Zan! she thought suddenly. Where's Zan? Painfully, Felicia sat up.

Zan and Nick stood a short distance away. Hugging.

"I hate her!" Zan screeched. "I'm going to kill her!"

Nick grabbed Zan by the shoulders and shook her. "Shut up, Zan!" he screamed. *"Just shut up!"*

Zan fell silent for a moment, her eyes wide and shocked. "Don't you tell me to shut up!" she yelled. "You care about her more than me!"

"I do not!" he snapped. "Why can't you believe me? Why can't you stop trying to hurt her? She's *nothing!* She means nothing to me!"

A lump rose in Felicia's throat. I'm all alone, she thought.

Zan collapsed in Nick's arms. "Don't lie to me, Nick," she moaned weakly.

"I'm not lying, Zan. I'm with you. Not Felicia. *You."*

Nick led Zan away without a glance at Felicia. He held her so close, kissing her cheek and stroking her hair.

Slowly, Felicia stood up. She ached all over, a deep pain that invaded every joint.

I have to run away again. I have to.

Zan will keep coming after me until I'm dead. And when the stories about the fire hit the news, I'll be way too easy for the Ridgely police to track down.

But what about Nick? a tiny voice inside her asked.

What about him? she thought. He's never going to leave Zan. He loves her. I could never be as important to him as she is. He doesn't even care that she tried to kill me.

Felicia's fingers tightened around Nick's car keys. She wouldn't be needing them after all.

She made her way to the car, pain shooting

through her body with every step. She unlocked the door, then stuck the keys in the glove compartment.

She slammed the door, leaving it unlocked. Then she set off into the darkness. Once she arrived at Dr. Jones's house she knew exactly what she would do. Load up her backpack, empty a whole bag of cat food for Miss Quiz, and make tracks.

She had run away before. She could do it again. I'm getting good at this, she thought.

Oh no! Dad's picture! It's at school! Felicia realized. She couldn't leave it there. It was the only picture of him she had. The only piece of her old life she had kept.

Felicia groaned. She would have to go to school first thing tomorrow morning and grab it. Don't talk to anyone, don't look at anyone, don't even think about it, she ordered herself. Just take the photo and get out.

Get as far away from Shadyside as possible. Before something bad happens. Something very bad.

chapter
21

"Kristy! Andy! Get out of the house!"

Felicia's friends didn't turn to face her. "You're going to die in there!" Felicia cried.

Slowly, Andy and Kristy turned toward Felicia. Kristy cradled her severed arm against her chest. Andy's face looked like raw hamburger.

"We're already dead, Felicia," Andy moaned through his torn, bloody lips. One of his teeth fell to the ground.

"You killed us. Why, Felicia? Why? We thought you were our friend," Kristy wailed. Tears of blood ran down her face.

They moved stiffly toward Felicia. She could smell their bodies beginning to decay.

"No!" Felicia shrieked. *"No!* I didn't mean to. I didn't mean to."

She jerked upright—and found herself in bed. A nightmare, she realized. A hideous nightmare.

Felicia's heartbeat hammered in her ears. I'm never going to forget what happened today. For the rest of my life I'll know that I killed Kristy and Andy.

She couldn't go back to sleep now. What if she dreamed again about destroying the house—and murdering her friends?

I wish I could talk to someone. Felicia glanced over at the clock. Nearly two in the morning. I can't call Debbie. And Aunt Margaret has been asleep for hours.

Felicia straightened her tangled sheet and stretched out on the bed again. Hot tears rolled down her cheeks.

I never wanted to hurt them. Never! Why did it have to be this way?

She closed her eyes. Immediately her mind filled with visions of the house collapsing. Nails flying. Boards crunching.

Kristy and Andy screaming.

Tap. Tap. Tap.

Felicia's eyes snapped open. What was that?

Tap. Tap. Tap.

Someone knocking on the window? A pale face stared at her through the glass.

Debbie!

Felicia jumped out of bed and gestured for Debbie to go around to the front door. She pulled on her robe and hurried down the hall.

"You have to leave town—tonight!" Debbie exclaimed the moment Felicia opened the door.

"Shhh!" Felicia warned. "Don't wake up Aunt Margaret." She led Debbie back to her room and shut the door behind them. "Why? What's wrong? What happened?" she demanded.

"I just spent the last four hours at the police station," Debbie replied. "They picked me up right after I got home. They think something is up."

Felicia stuffed her hands in the pockets of her robe. Suddenly she felt cold. "Why would they think that?"

"I don't know. But they do, and they kept asking me over and over again what happened! They think you had something to do with it!" Debbie whispered.

"That can't be!" Felicia moaned. "I mean, how could they think I knocked a whole house down?"

Debbie grabbed Felicia's arm and squeezed. "They kept asking me about the experiments at the lab. They're suspicious. There have been all kinds of rumors about the tests. *That's* why they picked me up."

Debbie hesitated. "They called Dr. Shanks. He told them everything, Felicia. They know about your power! They know your power is strong enough to rip down a house."

"Oh no!" she gasped. "What am I going to do, Debbie?"

"Pack a bag and get out of here. It's your only chance."

"Are you crazy?" Felicia protested. "Running just makes it look worse!"

"Felicia, they're going to come for you," Debbie answered, her voice grim. "They think you killed Andy and Kristy deliberately!"

"No. I have to turn myself in. Try to explain. You can tell them I didn't know anyone was inside. You can tell them it was an accident."

"I'm your best friend," Debbie replied. "They wouldn't believe me. Besides, they know about your powers—so they're going to think you're some kind of freak. They won't believe you're just a normal girl. They will think your powers make you dangerous—a killer."

Debbie turned and crossed to Felicia's closet. She pulled a backpack off the top shelf and tossed it onto the bed. "Start packing. I'm not going to let you stay here and get sent to jail for the rest of your life. You'll leave tonight in my car. That will give you a big head start. They'll never find you."

"You'd give me your car?" Felicia asked.

"I'll lend it to you," Debbie replied. "You drive it for a day, then leave it in a parking lot somewhere. Send me the keys and the directions. My brother and I will pick it up later. You've got to do it, Felicia. You've got to get out of here—before it's too late."

Felicia gazed into Debbie's eyes. She's afraid for me, she realized. Debbie is terrified.

"Oh, Debbie, how did this happen? I never meant to hurt Andy and Kristy."

Debbie nodded. "I know. But you can't sit around waiting for them to arrest you, Felicia. Come on."

Felicia took a deep breath and wiped her cheeks. It was now or never. "Okay, Deb, Let's do it."

Debbie grinned and stood. "I'll help you pack."

In less than five minutes, Felicia assembled a basic "survival kit"—some clothes, her favorite baseball cap, her portable tape player and several cassettes, and her father's picture. She shrugged on the backpack and paused for one last look at her bedroom.

She wanted to say goodbye to Aunt Margaret, but she knew she couldn't. Aunt Margaret would try to stop her.

"Come on," Debbie urged. "It's not safe for you here."

They hurried out to Debbie's car and headed out of Ridgely. They made one quick stop at a cash machine. Felicia withdrew her entire savings account. Only about three hundred dollars. She would need every penny.

"Did you leave a note?" Debbie asked as they pulled away from the bank.

"No," Felicia replied. "I couldn't bear to. I didn't know what to tell Aunt Margaret."

When they reached the town limits, Debbie pulled to the side of the road. The tree-lined street was dark and dead.

Debbie put the car in park and climbed out.

"Slide over," she told Felicia. "The car is all yours. For a day, anyway."

Felicia awkwardly crawled into the driver's seat. Her hands shook as she gripped the steering wheel. She glanced up at Debbie.

"You're scared," Debbie whispered.

"You think?" Felicia tried to joke. But her voice broke.

Debbie leaned in the window. "You *should* be afraid, Felicia. I think you should know, Dr. Shanks told the police you were out of control, a danger to other people. The police want you locked up."

Felicia stared at her best friend in horror.

"So *be* afraid," Debbie continued. "Make fear your best friend. Maybe it will keep you free."

A tear rolled down Felicia's cheek. "I don't know where to go," she muttered. "I'm *not* some dangerous monster. I don't know what to do."

Debbie reached in and placed her hand on Felicia's shoulder. "Don't worry about that right now. You don't have to decide where to go. Just drive as far as you can tonight. You'll figure it out soon enough."

"Thanks," Felicia whispered. "I don't know where I'd be without you, Deb."

"At home sleeping, probably," Debbie replied. She stared down at her feet, looking miserable. "I was the one who dared you to knock down the house, remember?"

"Yeah." Felicia shrugged. "But I did it."

"I'm sorry," Debbie replied softly. "I really, truly am sorry."

Felicia sniffled. "It's okay."

Debbie shook her head sadly. "I guess we're both going to have to live with what we did, huh?"

"I guess," Felicia replied, trying to sound strong.

They stared at each other for a long moment.

Finally, Debbie shrugged. "Don't make my car too hard to find."

"I promise."

"Be careful." Debbie stepped away from the car and began walking toward the opposite side of the road. She turned and waved to Felicia before she disappeared under the shadow of the trees.

Felicia waved back and rolled the window up against the cool night air. Again she tried to put her hands on the steering wheel, but they shook so violently that she had to make fists to stop the trembling.

Terror gripped her. What if the police tracked her down? What if they were searching for her that very minute?

But I didn't murder anyone! she thought desperately. I'm not a killer! It was only a horrible accident!

It's not fair that I have to run away because of this, she thought. I didn't ask for these powers!

Felicia froze. She felt a familiar sensation deep within her body. The same feeling she'd had that afternoon when the power surged from her mind into the beams of the old beach house.

Power. The power that filled her whenever she grew angry or upset.

No! she thought frantically. *Not now! Not now!*

The car shook, rocking from side to side. The glove compartment door flew open. Papers, pens, and maps spilled onto the front seat. The radio snapped on, the tuner spinning from one end of the dial to the other. The volume flipped to high, blasting static-filled music that nearly blew the speakers.

"No!" Felicia screamed. "Debbie! Help me!"

But Debbie was gone. Felicia was all alone.

The tires left the pavement with every shake of the car, slamming Felicia into the door again and again. She could feel the wheels rising higher off the ground each time. The car would flip in seconds!

The engine raced. The gas pedal hit the floor. The tires spun. The gear shift began to move.

Then Felicia smelled it.

Gas.

Get out, her mind roared. *Get out now!*

Felicia grabbed her backpack and yanked the door handle.

It didn't budge.

Her mind whirled. Was her power holding the door shut?

What's going on?

The gas smell grew thicker. Felicia began to cough. All it would take was one spark. . . .

Then she spotted it—the lock on the door pushed all the way down. Relief flooded Felicia. She fumbled for the lock. Pulled it up. She kicked open the heavy door and threw herself from the car.

Safe, Felicia thought.

I'm safe.

A violent roar exploded in her ears. Bright orange flames blinded her.

A blast of hot air slammed into Felicia, lifting her off the ground.

Felicia flew through the air as Debbie's car blew up.

chapter
22

*F*elicia landed hard on her hands and knees. Luckily she landed in the tall grass at the side of the road.

She waited for the pain to fade. Blinking hard, she stared at the burning car. Finally, she dragged herself to her feet. She sprinted into the woods and didn't stop running until she hit the interstate.

I can't let them catch me, she thought. First the beach house, now Debbie's car. My powers really *are* out of control.

If they catch me, they'll lock me up forever. It was the only thought that kept her running. . . .

Now it was time for her to run again. Time to leave Shadyside. Time to leave Nick.

Stop thinking of him, Felicia scolded herself as

she turned onto Fear Street. There's nothing in Shadyside for you anymore.

Nick didn't care about her. Zan wanted to kill her. Felicia finally knew how to control her powers—how to use them for good. But that only made people want to put her face on TV for the police to see.

Felicia ran up the steps to Dr. Jones's house, then slammed and locked the door behind her. It took only five minutes to pack up her stuff. She thought about just taking off tonight, right now.

No, she thought. I can't leave without Dad's picture. It's all I have left.

Felicia slept on the living-room couch. From there she could see if a car pulled into the driveway during the night. If the police came, she would run straight out the back door and keep running.

The sunlight woke Felicia. Miss Quiz slept on her lap, purring softly. Dr. Jones's house was silent.

No police, Felicia realized. No one came after me.

Not even Nick.

Felicia stood up and pulled her baseball cap on. Time for school, she thought. Time to go to Shadyside High one last time.

Just get the picture, she told herself as she walked. Don't talk to anyone.

She slipped through the front doors of the high school a few minutes early. The halls were just starting to fill up.

Students buzzed back and forth in her path. Felicia ignored them all. She stared at the ground as she walked. Finally she reached her locker.

She started to work the combination lock— when a hand clutched her arm and yanked her roughly to the side.

chapter

23

*F*elicia let out a scream.

She turned and swung her fist as hard as she could. A heavy hand clamped over her mouth. The other hand pushed her back against the locker.

"Calm down, Felicia! It's only me."

Nick!

He moved his hand away from her mouth. "Sorry I scared you. I just want to talk."

"Are you kidding?" she cried. "Let go of me!" Felicia tried to shove him away.

He tightened his grip on her arm. "No. I have to talk to you. I'm not going to let you go now!"

Nick slid his arms around her, pulled her close—and kissed her. Felicia was too shocked to struggle. All the anger she had felt melted away.

She threw her arms around him and kissed him back.

Finally, Nick broke away. He gazed into her eyes.

"Felicia, I'm so sorry about last night," he told her. "I didn't mean what I said to Zan. You're not nothing. You mean *everything* to me."

"Oh, Nick," she whispered. "I feel the same way."

"Whew," he replied. *"That's* good."

"Nick, there's something I—"

"If it's Zan you're worried about, don't," he said quickly. "She and I had a long talk last night. She promised to see a shrink, Felicia. She promised never to hurt you again. You're safe."

"Did you break up with her?" Felicia asked.

Nick's eyes darted away, and Felicia knew immediately that Nick had not.

"Nick . . ."

"I couldn't do it, okay?" he cried. "So much happened last night. And she promised so much. She really wants to change, Felicia. I couldn't hurt her anymore."

Felicia scowled. Unbelievable, she thought. Nick is trying to keep us both at the same time!

For one brief moment when Nick had kissed her, she thought she might still have a future in Shadyside.

But not now.

"Felicia," Nick pleaded. "I still want us to be together."

"No, Nick," she replied firmly. "It's too late. I

can't be with you as long as Zan is around. So today I'm going—"

A shrill screech cut off Felicia's words. She spun around—and froze.

Zan came charging down the hall toward Felicia, a knife raised in her hand!

chapter

24

Felicia heard other kids scream. Kids were running in all directions, a blur of panic.

But Felicia couldn't drag her eyes away from the knife.

Nick jumped in front of Zan and raised his hands.

"Zan!" he cried. "What are you—"

He shrieked in pain as Zan whipped the knife across his outstretched hands. Felicia watched the razor-sharp edge biting into his left palm. Nick fell back, clutching the hand to his chest. Blood leaked through his fingers in small rivers.

"Nick!" Felicia cried. She heard more screams, someone yelling for the principal.

Zan tackled her.

She grabbed Felicia, spinning her around and

yanking her head back by her hair. Felicia's baseball cap flew to the floor. She threw her hands up to protect her throat from the knife.

Zan hacked at Felicia's fists.

Felicia yelped when the blade bit into her right arm.

Zan placed the blade against her throat. "Don't you dare do that again!" she snarled.

"Zan, let her go!" Nick screamed, gripping his bloody hand. "You promised!"

Zan laughed. "Are you kidding, Nick? I was just lying—the way you do. *Both* of you. How long have you been going behind my back, Nick? Since the day she hitched into town?"

"It doesn't matter what I do," Nick replied. "You only want to hurt people. If it wasn't Felicia, it would be someone else. You need help!"

"At least I never lie!" Zan growled.

"What about Doug Gaynor?" Felicia blurted out. "You lied about killing him."

"Who told you that!" Zan screamed.

The knife point scraped against Felicia's throat.

"Who?" Zan repeated.

"I figured it out myself!" Felicia screamed back. "I saw the bloody page in your yearbook!"

"Of course I killed him!" Zan shrieked. "He hurt me. So I hurt him back. Do you know what it's like to watch someone realize they're about to die? I stood on that balcony for fifteen minutes watching Doug die. He kept trying to say he was sorry. Can you believe that? I mean, he was just a little late with that apology, you know?"

Nick took a step forward.

"Back off," Zan ordered. "I'll cut her."

"Don't hurt her," Nick pleaded.

"I might," Zan threatened. "I might hurt her a lot."

Felicia tried to ignore the knife at her throat. She reached down inside, searching for the power she felt last night. Energy surged through her, filling her mind. Rushing through her body.

"Zan?" she asked gently.

"What?"

"Did you send me the note?"

Zan laughed again. "Yes. *And* I painted my message on the wall. If you had done the smart thing and left town, none of this would be happening. I'm so *sick* of being hurt by people I love! I even liked *you*, Felicia, for about twenty seconds. Then I saw the way you stared at Nick. And I knew you had to die. So get ready!"

Zan snarled and raised the knife again.

Felicia unleashed the power, throwing everything she had at Zan.

The plate glass windows up and down the hallway exploded inward in a terrifying spray of razor-sharp glass. Lockers rattled on their hinges, threatening to tear loose from the wall.

"What are you doing?" Zan demanded. "What is this?"

"This is the real me!" Felicia declared.

Zan's face twisted. "Bye bye, runaway," she grunted.

The point of the knife pierced Felicia's throat.

Now or never, Felicia thought.

The power surged, aimed like a laser beam—

directly at the knife point. The sharp tip curled backwards, tucking under itself.

Felicia pushed with all of her might, screaming as the blade rolled up. The steel squealed in protest. Zan gasped at the curled weapon in her hand.

Before Zan could recover her senses, Felicia lashed out again. She formed a picture in her mind and made it come true.

Zan screamed as Felicia's power lifted her into the air.

Felicia scrambled up. Staggered to the wall—and faced her.

Zan hung several feet off the ground, her feet and arms pinwheeling crazily.

"What are you doing?" Zan screamed. "You're some kind of freak!"

Felicia replied by hurling Zan backward. Zan slammed into a bank of lockers and hung there, suspended three feet off the ground.

"I'll kill you—you freak!" Zan roared. "Let me down!"

"Hold her," Felicia ordered.

Nick ran forward and struggled to grab Zan. His injured hand left a trail of blood on the floor.

Two boys rushed forward to help Nick hold Zan's arms, pressing her against the lockers until help could arrive.

Felicia felt her power start to trickle out of her. She stopped concentrating, and the power faded away.

Zan slid down the wall to the floor. The boys held her down.

She screamed threats, but Felicia hardly heard

them. Her mind whirled. She gazed down at the knife on the floor.

I saved myself with my mind, Felicia thought numbly.

She *could* control the power! The fire at the hamburger restaurant tested it. The knife proved it.

Felicia touched the wound on her neck. Her fingers came away red with blood, but the cut wasn't bad. The one on her forearm was worse— her sleeve was soaked with blood.

Loud voices down the hall reminded Felicia that the police were probably coming for Zan.

Time to go, she thought. Get what you came for and run.

Felicia ran to her locker and spun the combination. She yanked down her father's picture and slid it into her inside jacket pocket. She gave her locker a quick once-over, and decided there was nothing from her days at Shadyside High that she wanted to keep.

As the principal and several teachers jogged down the hall toward Zan, Felicia grabbed up her baseball cap. She pulled it low over her face and sprinted for the front doors.

It's over, she thought.

I'm leaving Shadyside forever.

Felicia never thought she could be so happy to see Fear Street. Dr. Jones's house looked quiet and safe, especially after what happened at school.

She jogged across the front lawn, checking the handkerchief she had tied around the cut in her forearm. The bleeding had almost stopped. All the running probably didn't help, but she had no choice. She had to get out of Shadyside before the police found out where she was staying.

Felicia flung open the door and hurried inside.

This is it, she thought. Follow your plan, Felicia. Grab your backpack, dump some food for Miss Quiz, and get out.

Felicia knew the cat would be okay. Dr. Jones wasn't due back for weeks. But Bobby, the college kid who was supposed to watch Miss Quiz, would be back any day. Still, it was hard to leave the cat behind. As Felicia pulled the front door closed, she could hear her meowing inside.

Felicia dug in her jeans pocket for the key to lock the door. She planned to leave that in the mailbox for Bobby.

One of the boards on the porch creaked.

Felicia froze. Why would the wood creak . . . unless someone stepped on it?

Someone grabbed her arm!

Felicia screamed. Zan! Zan had escaped and come after her!

Felicia twisted away and prepared to defend herself.

chapter

25

"*D*ebbie!" Felicia exclaimed. "What are you doing here?"

Felicia dropped her backpack onto the porch and threw her arms around her old friend.

Debbie pushed her away. Felicia stumbled backward and stared at her in surprise. Then she noticed the expression on Debbie's face.

"Debbie . . . what's wrong?" Felicia whispered. "Why are you here? Did something happen to Aunt Margaret?"

"Guess what I saw on the news last night?" Debbie replied. "Some grease pit burned to the ground in a town called Shadyside. But one brave girl risked her life to rescue her co-workers and customers."

Felicia stiffened. The fire! She had made the news after all.

"The weird thing," Debbie continued, "is the way the brave girl fought the flames. No one could really explain it. And of course the brave girl couldn't be reached for comment. One witness said it was as if she *willed* the flames back."

Debbie's eyes were filled with malice.

"You couldn't resist it, could you?" she asked. "You had to be the great American heroine. Well, now everyone knows who you are, Felicia. Everyone knows about your precious powers."

"D-Debbie," Felicia stammered. "What's going on? Why are you saying these things?"

"Because it makes me sick!" Debbie snapped. "You can't even disappear without messing it up. Everyone wants to hunt you down, Felicia. All I can say is, I'm glad I found you first."

"Why?" Felicia demanded.

Debbie's mouth twisted into a sneer. "Because I'm going to kill you. And this time I'm going to do it right!"

chapter
26

"Kill me?" Felicia choked out. "*Why?*"

She retreated until her shoulders bumped the front door. She had nowhere else to go.

"Because I thought you were dead already," Debbie explained angrily. "But I messed up. I thought you were in my car when it exploded!"

Felicia's mind whirled. "That's impossible. How could you know my powers were going to fly out of control and blow up your car?"

"They didn't!" Debbie growled. "In fact, they probably saved you! No flames burned you. No chunks of steel ripped you apart. When you landed, nothing was broken. Anyone else would have been cut in half by that explosion."

"Then how did the car explode?" Felicia asked weakly.

Debbie narrowed her eyes at Felicia. *"I* did that. *I* made it explode. You're so wrapped up in yourself that you never figured out *I* have telekinetic powers, too. I have always had them. And mine are even greater than the great Felicia's."

Felicia felt numb. She didn't understand what Debbie was telling her. Debbie *did* have powers?

That's why she stayed at the Ridgely lab for so long, Felicia realized.

"Don't look so shocked," Debbie snapped. "I was always a better liar than you. I had enough sense not to let the whole world know about my powers. All you could do was whine about how the power was ruining your life."

Felicia began moving slowly along the front wall of the house. "I don't care if you have powers," she said. "I never cared. You were the one who seemed so jealous."

"I'm not jealous of you!" Debbie replied. "Your powers are nothing. But you were too much of a risk after the beach house.

"I couldn't let anyone find out the truth about what happened. I lied. I never talked to the cops that night. Neither did Dr. Shanks. But I couldn't take the chance that you might tell them later on. Little Miss Guilty Conscience and all."

"Debbie, I don't get it," Felicia pleaded. *"What are you talking about?"*

"I loved Andy Murray!" Debbie cried. "You were so into your miserable life at Ridgely that you never knew. I thought he cared about me, too. But

137

he didn't know I was alive. I couldn't get him away from Kristy. He just walked away from me. But my plan was perfect. Neither of them escaped."

"Plan?" Felicia choked out.

"Andy and Kristy went to that old beach house all the time. It was their favorite spot. They always thought they were alone, but I watched them. I figured they should die there, since they liked it so much. I brought you along that day to help me. I wasn't sure I could make that whole house collapse by myself. I never moved anything that big before."

"You used me for murder!" Felicia cried. "You're insane!"

"I'm *brilliant,*" Debbie replied. "But I learned one thing from you, Felicia."

"What's that?"

"That I didn't need you as much as I thought. Your tiny powers barely made a dent in that house. It was all me." Debbie crossed her arms. "And now it's time for the little runaway to stop running. *For good.*"

Felicia's power charged through her veins. Even after her run-in with Zan, Felicia still felt strong. She knew more about controlling her power than ever before.

But was it enough to beat Debbie?

Try, she told herself.

She lashed out at Debbie—and Felicia heard a loud smack. Debbie fell back, holding her cheek.

"What was that?" Debbie demanded.

"The slap in the face you deserve!" Felicia cried.

Debbie let out a roar of rage. She flung her hands

out—and Felicia flew up off the porch floor. Felicia hit the roof of the porch. The wood splintered against her back. Air whooshed out of her lungs, and she hung there the same way Zan had against the lockers.

Debbie *was* strong!

Felicia lashed out again, blowing Debbie off the porch with a powerful, invisible current. Debbie landed on her back on the front lawn.

Felicia felt the invisible hand release her. She fell to the porch, gasping for air.

Before she could regain her balance, the porch exploded from under her. She felt weightless as she flew over the lawn in a blizzard of wood splinters and rusty nails.

She hit the ground hard. But for the first time, Felicia actually felt her power protect her from the impact.

Get up! an inner voice commanded. *Fight her!*

Debbie was too fast. She tore loose a massive tree branch from one of the big maples on the front lawn, her mind swinging it at Felicia like a bat.

Felicia had no time to duck. Instinctively, she reached out to the nearest object—a six-foot light pole near the driveway—and yanked it from the ground. It came loose with a groan and met Debbie's tree limb head-on. The shock waves sent Debbie reeling backwards. The tree limb dropped to the lawn.

Felicia moved in for the kill.

She hurled the twisted, ruined end of the light pole at Debbie like a spear.

Debbie rolled to the side with a grunt. The light pole dug into the grass harmlessly, sticking out of the dirt like a javelin.

"Nice try!" Debbie taunted. She glanced away from Felicia for a second, her eyes betraying her next target: Dr. Jones's recycling trash can.

Oh no, Felicia thought.

The garbage can flipped on its side. An avalanche of cans and bottles poured out, firing off like fastballs.

"No!" Felicia screamed, throwing her power out recklessly, without thinking.

A thick Coke bottle shattered on Felicia's skull, bringing a blinding pain with it. She fell to her knees, holding up her arms to shield her from the rest of Debbie's attack.

Blood leaked into her left eye. Felicia howled as glass shattered all around her. Cans clattered. Plastic bottles crumpled.

Yet she felt nothing but the pain of that first bottle.

Finally, the barrage stopped.

Felicia lowered her arms and wiped blood out of her eye.

She gasped. Broken bottles and torn aluminum cans covered the lawn in a ten-foot circle around her. But only one had hit her!

The power, she thought. It saved me again.

Felicia staggered to her feet. A wave of nausea rolled over her and she sank back down. Debbie stood in front of her, an expression of triumph on her face.

"It's not like in the movies, is it?" Debbie called.

"What?" Felicia mumbled.

"Bottles hurt when they shatter on your head."

A drop of blood ran into Felicia's mouth. She gagged as another strong wave of nausea made her grab her stomach. She couldn't fight anymore. She had nothing left.

"You're stronger than I thought, Felicia," Debbie admitted. "But I'm even stronger. The only thing to figure out now is *how* to kill you. I see a shovel over there—I could hit you with it. Or maybe I'll just break your neck. Which do you prefer?"

Felicia gazed blurrily up at Debbie. She didn't reply.

"Okay," Debbie decided. "The shovel it is."

The squealing of tires distracted them both. Felicia turned in the direction of the sound—and spotted Nick's car screeching around the corner.

"Who's that?" Debbie demanded.

Felicia's heart pounded. She didn't reply.

Nick jumped out of his car and stared at the destruction—the porch, the tree, the garbage.

"Felicia!" he cried, charging up the lawn.

Debbie turned quickly to the steel mailbox by the driveway. The mailbox squealed and tore loose from its pole.

"No!" Felicia screamed, watching it fly at Nick's head.

She reached down inside her. And threw all her rage, all her fear, and all her frustration outward. Felicia flung her hands toward Debbie, as if passing a basketball.

The power flowed out. But this was something different.

Felicia aimed this last bit of her power not at a tree or a bottle, but at Debbie's mind itself.

She felt the power rush out of her, down her arms and out her fingertips. "Oh!" Debbie uttered a startled cry. Her head jerked back as if struck. Her arms went limp at her sides. Her jaw hung open.

Debbie's eyes rolled back into her skull, showing only dull, bloodshot whites. A thin trickle of blood dribbled from Debbie's ears.

Debbie swayed for several seconds, her face blank, her mouth hanging open. Then, without uttering another sound, she pitched forward onto the lawn.

chapter

27

"**Y**ou know," Nick said as he fiddled with the car radio, "even though Debbie wanted to kill you, I'm glad you didn't kill her."

"Me too," Felicia replied. The countryside flew by so quickly outside the car window. They would arrive at Ridgely College within the hour. "Maybe it was my power working subconciously again. I only hit her hard enough to shock her mind, but not kill her."

"Has she come out of the coma yet?" Nick asked.

"It's not a coma," Felicia explained. "The doctors said it's more like a trance. They've never seen anything like it before. They think it's because of her power."

"Maybe her power saved her from yours," Nick replied.

"Could be. Time will tell, I guess."

"I guess," Nick agreed. "I just hope they don't put her in the same room with Zan at the institution."

Felicia shook her head. "Nick, that's *awful*. I hope they both get the help they need."

"I'm sorry you have to go back to Ridgely," Nick said quietly, changing the subject.

Felicia smiled, touching the stitches above her eye where the bottle had hit her. "Actually, I'm kind of looking forward to it. I called Aunt Margaret, and we had a long talk. She really cares about me. I guess I always knew that deep down. But she explained she only forced me into the testing with Dr. Shanks because she thought it would help me deal with my power. She said my father resisted testing more than I did."

"Like father, like daughter, huh?" Nick mused.

"I guess. Anyway, I want to learn as much as I can about my powers and where they came from. I've got a new attitude, you know? I don't feel like such a freak anymore. I don't think the doctors will be bullying me very much either."

"I can't believe they let Debbie go wild like that," Nick said, shaking his head.

"It's not their fault," Felicia replied. "She fooled everyone."

"Man, I'll never forget that mailbox flying at my head. That was so weird!"

"You're lucky it didn't brain you!" Felicia exclaimed.

"Thanks to you." Nick smiled tenderly. "You saved me."

Felicia returned the smile. "I owed you."

"Does that make us even?" he asked.

"On one condition. You come up and visit me every weekend."

"And if I don't?" Nick challenged.

"I broke out of there once before," Felicia reminded him playfully. "Don't think I won't hunt you down, Nick."

"You won't have to. I promise that you'll never, ever have to run away again."

Felicia grinned and rested her head on his shoulder, content to leave it there all the way back to Ridgely.

About the Author

"Where do you get your ideas?"

That's the question that R. L. Stine is asked most often. "I don't know where my ideas come from," he says. "But I do know that I have a lot more scary stories in my mind that I can't wait to write."

So far, he has written over a hundred mysteries and thrillers for young people, all of them bestsellers.

Bob grew up in Columbus, Ohio. Today he lives in an apartment near Central Park in New York City with his wife, Jane, and son, Matt.

THE NIGHTMARES
NEVER END . . .
WHEN YOU VISIT

Next . . .
KILLER'S KISS
(Coming mid-January 1997)

Delia and Karina compete over everything. Grades, popularity, an art scholarship—and Vincent. Both girls are determined to have Vincent for a boyfriend, no matter what.

Then Vincent ends up dead—with a purple lipstick print on his cheek. Is the lipstick Delia's or Karina's? Which girl was willing to kill for love?

Now your younger brothers or sisters
can take a walk down Fear Street....

R·L·STINE'S
GHOSTS OF FEAR STREET ®

1 Hide and Shriek   52941-2/$3.99
2 Who's Been Sleeping in My Grave? 52942-0/$3.99
3 Attack of the Aqua Apes   52943-9/$3.99
4 Nightmare in 3-D   52944-7/$3.99
5 Stay Away From the Tree House 52945-5/$3.99
6 Eye of the Fortuneteller   52946-3/$3.99
7 Fright Knight   52947-1/$3.99
8 The Ooze   52948-X/$3.99
9 Revenge of the Shadow People   52949-8/$3.99
10 The Bugman Lives   52950-1/$3.99
11 The Boy Who Ate Fear Street   00183-3/$3.99
12 Night of the Werecat   00184-1/$3.99
13 How to be a Vampire   00185-X/$3.99
14 Body Switchers from Outer Space
                                                   00186-8/$3.99
15 Fright Christmas   00187-6/$3.99
16 Don't Ever get Sick at Granny's 00188-4/$3.99

A MINSTREL BOOK

FEAR STREET®

R L STINE